FIRST KILL

Gambler Matt Wilson had often wondered how he'd feel if a man lifted a gun against him to kill him. Right now he was about to find out.

His words rang up and down the street. "Sooner or later you'll force yourself to pull your gun, Applegate. So why not do it now?"

Applegate went into his gunman's crouch. Both splayed hands went down, hit gun butts. Both guns rose. He was fast, all right, much faster than Wilson. But what paralyzed Wilson's hand was his reluctance to shoot at another man with intent to kill.

GUNSMOKE GAMBLER

Wade Hamilton

LEISURE BOOKS ⮂ NEW YORK CITY

A LEISURE BOOK

Published by

Nordon Publications, Inc.
Two Park Avenue
New York, N.Y. 10016

GUNSMOKE
GAMBLER

Chapter One

On this day, Matt Wilson saw a man murdered.

The buckboard stood in an alley. Beside it, two men were talking. Then one turned to untie the team and the other man murdered him.

Neither man saw Wilson, who had entered the alley behind them at that moment, for the gambler was taking a short-cut from the town's livery stable.

Wilson stopped with the brutality of this scene, the terror of it, curdling his blood, pounding against his heart. He saw the killer deliberately put his .45 against the man's back.

He saw the gun-hammer fall. He heard the muffled roar.

The slug tore through the man's heart. Wilson saw the man sag, grab for the nearest horse, then fall to the ground and lie still, face down.

And the killer, his back still toward Wilson, reached down and took the murdered man's pistol out of its holster. Unperturbed, he placed the pistol beside the dead man's hand.

Out on the street, men called. Boots sounded. Despite the drenching heat of the Montana July afternoon, Sageville had come to life. Sageville was converging on this alley.

Then the killer turned. For the first time, he saw Matt Wilson. His eyes, dark, small and evil, moved over

Matt Wilson's tough six-foot frame.

They took in Wilson's neat blue suit, the pant-legs stuck into polished Hyer boots. They probed Wilson's face—thin, angular and with harsh planes, tough contours. They stood still on Wilson's face.

"Who the hell are you, stranger?"

"Matt Wilson."

"Gambler."

Wilson's blue eyes locked the assassin's dark, evil eyes. Wilson wished he'd not had the bad luck to stumble across this murder. What they did in this high Montana Territory town meant no never-mind to him. Hell, they could shoot and kill each other all they wanted. It was none of his business.

He'd only come to visit his only brother, Jim.

"You asked me my name. I ask you yours."

"Rand Johnson. How long you been standin' there, gambler?"

"I just came around the corner."

"When?"

Wilson said: "The man there was on the ground. His pistol lay beside him. I judge you two had a gunfight."

"H'ain't never seen you aroun' Sageville before. You come to gamble here?"

"My business, Johnson. None of yours."

Rand Johnson's beefy face reddened. "Right smart with your tongue, gambler."

Wilson felt resentment rise. He was tired of the saddle, of the long trail. He needed a bath, a shave. He was hungry.

He glanced down at the dead man. All blood had drained from the man's face. When the man had fallen, his face had been tan and high of color. Now it was very white.

Wilson's glance held nothing but mild curiosity. He'd seen a few other dead men in his twenty-six years.

He looked back at Rand Johnson.

Suspicion and distrust lay naked and ugly in the wide face of this broad-shouldered assassin. Rand Johnson

8

didn't know for sure whether or not Wilson had seen him murder this man.

Rand Johnson wanted to make sure.

"When you got here—he was down? You never saw him pull against me, gambler?"

Wilson shook his head.

Johnson breathed deeply. He looked about at the assembled townspeople. Wilson said: "You're full of questions."

"I wanted a witness," Johnson said. "I wanted a witness, to testify that Smith reached first."

Wilson looked at Rand Johnson. "Do you think I'm lying? Are you calling me a liar?"

"No, but—"

"What difference would it have made if I'd got here earlier and seen the gunfight?" Wilson asked.

He had Johnson momentarily cornered. This showed in the man's coarse, thick-lipped face, the hard intake of harsh breath. Then Johnson saw his way out.

"This man here is a farmer," he pointed out. "Farmers are strong around here. I could use a witness to tell how I shot in self-defense."

"I'm not your witness. I didn't see the gunfight."

Wilson judged every soul in Sageville surrounded them now. Out of the crowd came a deep voice: "Are you sure, stranger?"

Wilson saw a bony, big-handed man wearing a blacksmith's leather apron. Faded blue eyes regarded Wilson under craggy brows.

"What's it to you?" Wilson asked.

A thick tongue wet thick lips. "This is a troubled range, stranger— a range of sudden, violent death. And this dead man was a farmer named Horace Smith—a simple, God-fearing man of the soil. He was no gunman."

"He pulled against me," Johnson said. "He cursed me. He reached for his gun. He even got it out of holster. There it is, beside his hand. Leave this stranger out of this, savvy? Shoot your questions at me—not

9

him. My gun kilt Smith, not his'n!"

Matt Wilson had seen—and heard—enough.

He started to leave. The blacksmith said: "I'd be pleased if you stayed a while, sir."

Wilson stopped. He stood. He waited.

Wilson looked again at the dead man. A townsman had rolled him on his back, and was brushing dust from the man's face.

Wilson idly noted that Rand Johnson evidently shot steel-jacketed bullets, for the hole in the dead man's chest where the bullet had come out was the same size as the one on his back where the bullet had entered.

A coroner's jury would think the bullet had entered from the front. Only Rand Johnson—and a gambler named Matt Wilson— knew that Smith had been shot in the back.

And Johnson wasn't sure whether Wilson had seen the murder or not, and therefore Matt Wilson's life was in danger. It was that simple, that elemental, Wilson realized.

Now the big blacksmith stoutly said: "I was talkin' to this gambler here—not you, Johnson." His next words went in Wilson's direction. "If you saw this gunman— this hired killer—murder this farmer, speak up and let us know, so he'll have to answer to a court of law—and to the higher court of God Almighty."

If he meant to say more, his words were chopped short by Rand Johnson's rising right fist. It caught the blacksmith flush on the mouth.

Johnson's blow was so unexpected that the blacksmith went back against the buggy, hit a wheel, and sat down hard. He was dazed, but not out. Blood oozed from his battered nose.

"When you talk to me," Rand Johnson said, "call me *sir*—savvy?"

The blacksmith spat blood. Rand Johnson whirled and looked hard at Wilson again. Wilson met the assassin's gaze, and cynicism curled his lips slightly. This man, with his limited intelligence, was dangerous. He struck unexpectedly, shot from behind.

Wilson said ironically: "Think you'll know me the next time you see me, Johnson?" His tone was an insult.

Johnson studied him. Wilson knew that Johnson was still trying to figure him out. He heard the gunman's slow intake of measured breath. Color crawled up Johnson's cheekbones to his small eyes, his lips drew back harshly.

With a noncommittal shrug, Wilson turned away toward Main Street.

The high Montana sun, hot with the terrible July heat of 1888, beat against the parched earth, giving the warped and painted buildings a sinister appearance.

He'd stay in this jerkwater burg long. Just long enough to have a good visit with brother Jim, and then he'd ride out.

This town had trouble. He wanted none of it.

Chapter Two

Matt Wilson came to Main Street, his cynical smile still playing. Main was Sageville's one and only street—two blocks long, north and south.

Boot-worn plank sidewalks fronted the frame buildings. Tooth-gnawed cottonwood hitching rails and posts. Dust and gravel. Even the proverbial bony cur, slinking.

Matt Wilson thought of Rio de Janeiro.

Winter—or what Brazilians called winter—was in full sway, down below the Equator.

Winter time?

Matt Wilson smiled. Warm weather there, not too hot, not too chilly. Gay, laughing crowds. Blacks and whites, and no color hatred.

The warm, friendly ocean. Yes, and Sugarloaf Mountain, Copacabana with its golden sands. Blue sunlight dancing and sparkling on blue water.

A man should go where the weather fits his clothes. And a gambler could go and make a living where he wanted, as long as he kept his wits nimble and his fingers fast and supple.

He'd winter in Rio again.

But first he'd visit Jim. Why did Jim stay in this godforsaken country? Boiling heat in the summer, forty below zero blizzards come winter. Well, each man to his own pumpkin, and—

"Hey, you, there!"

The harsh voice came from behind. Wilson paid it no attention. He was nobody's dog. He was not at the beck and call of this burg.

"Hey, you, there—hey, gambler!"

Wilson frowned, and turned.

A man had followed him onto Main Street. Wilson remembered seeing him close to Johnson. He instantly disliked him.

Plainly the man was arrogant, bossy. His harsh voice, his authoritative bearing, told Wilson this.

Wilson had met his type before—many times. Wry distaste touched Wilson's tongue.

"You calling me?"

"You said you were a gambler. And you can hear, can't you?"

Wilson's brows rose. He had an ironic thought: this man figured he'd live forever.

"What do you want? And who are you?" Wilson asked.

The man stopped beside Wilson. Wilson judged him to be in his middle thirties. He was wide, heavy-set, broad, muscular. A double-breasted brown coat covered wide shoulders.

The coat was buttoned, even in this heat.

His face was wide, clean-shaven. Deep sideburns decorated heavy jowls. A gold watch-chain spanned his barrel chest.

"Bart Corcoran's my name," said the man.

Wilson had had too much. Cynicism came surging. "Bart Corcoran, huh? What am I supposed to do? Dance a jig? Get on my knees in the dust? Just think— I've met *Bart Corcoran!*"

Corcoran's dark eyes darkened dangerously. Plainly, he'd not expected this. His lips twisted angrily.

Somewhere, a woman laughed.

Wilson looked at the woman. She had come from the drug store two doors up-street. She stopped.

Wilson's eyes met hers. Her eyes met Wilson's. Wil-

14

son liked what he saw. His heart beat quicker.

The woman looked at Corcoran.

Her lips showed scorn.

Wilson watched her, completely disregarding Bart Corcoran. He spoke to God and to Matt Wilson. "God's most wonderful gift to man . . . . "

Corcoran scowled. He looked at the woman, then at Wilson. His scowl grew. Did this gambler have his full mental faculties? Talking to himself on a public street?

Again, Wilson's thoughts were on Marie— Marie, who was now forever gone. Somewhere, a cold wind blew. The crown of the hill was cold. Marie was dead.

"Her name, Corcoran?"

"Whose name, gambler?"

"The lady there."

"Oh, Jean Benson. Why ask?"

"Just a question."

The woman paused in the doorway of the Sageville Cafe. She was too far away to overhear. She again looked at Matt Wilson, who judged her in her early twenties.

Their eyes met. Her sea-blue eyes were calm. Wilson nodded. She did not return his nod.

She entered the cafe. Wilson's heart settled down, and he looked back at the overbearing Bart Corcoran.

"What do you want, Corcoran?" Wilson repeated.

"Rand Johnson rides for me."

"Rides?"

"I own Bar Six iron, only big ranch around here. I run over twenty thousand head. Farmers are movin' in on my grass. That farmer Johnson had to kill to protect his own life—"

Wilson nodded. He knew that bothered Corcoran. Wilson felt an invisible met tighten around him.

Luck, bad luck—

Not good luck. Not Wilson's luck. Not the doing of Wilson's Man. Wilson's Man—always good luck.

Unfortunate timing . . . .

Now Corcoran prodded. "You saw the killing?"

Wilson summoned patience. "You heard me back there when I told your smithy I didn't see the gunfight. Don't push me, Corcoran."

"A threat, Wilson?"

"Call it what you want. Good day."

Wilson turned away.

The big hand came down. It landed hard on Wilson's left shoulder. Wilson stopped. He did not turn. He studied the hand—hairy, strong, fingers gripping.

His eyes moved over the hand. They encountered the dark eyes of Bart Corcoran.

"Take your hand from my shoulder, Corcoran."

Corcoran said: "Get outta town, gambler."

"I might. I might not."

"We don't want you. We don't need gamblers, any more than we need sodbusters."

People had left the alley. They watched. They stood in the dust. They stood on the planks. They stood watching.

"This is my town, Wilson. So get out, *tinhorn*!"

The word *tinhorn* did it.

It was not the hard grip on his shoulder. It was not the naked arrogance. It was the word *tinhorn*.

Wilson breathed deeply. A tinhorn was a crooked gambler. He marked cards, loaded dice. He cheated in every possible way. Brakes on roulette wheels.

He thought of his Twenty-One table in *Cuidad de Mejico*. Sleek women bending over cards. Tailored men with millions behind them.

And Monte Carlo . . . . and Hong Kong . . . . and Buenos Aires . . . . He expelled his breath.

Again he said: "Take your hand free."

The fingers tightened instead.

Then Wilson hit.

He had hit his share of men. He hit Corcoran as hard as he'd hit the others. He hit with his right.

His knuckles smashed Corcoran in the mouth. One blow sent Corcoran reeling back. Corcoran sat on the planks.

16

And Matt Wilson flexed his fingers and thought: I hope I didn't break a bone. I should have used my gun. Buffaloed him, not hit him.

His knuckles were skinned. No fingers broken. He breathed relief. He looked down at Bart Corcoran.

Corcoran's right hand went down, back—then stopped. Wilson's .45 covered him.

"Be careful."

Corcoran spoke through bloody lips. "My handkerchief, no more. My back pocket."

"Somebody give him a handkerchief."

A woman said: "I wouldn't give the sonofabitch the time of day! And that goes for Johnson too."

She was a stocky, high-breasted, middle-aged housewife. A man said: "Here, he can use my bandana."

The man—plainly a cowboy—untied his neckscarf. He handed it to Bart Corcoran, who threw it into the dust.

"Stinks," Corcoran said.

The cowpoke grinned good-naturedly, picked up his neckscarf, jammed it into his hind pocket.

Corcoran shook his big head, dark eyes clearing. He looked up at Matt Wilson.

"You hit hard, gambler—and sudden."

"The word *tinhorn*." Wilson said.

Hate glistened in Corcoran's eyes. His mouth worked, but he said nothing. Rand Johnson had moved in behind his boss.

Johnson's ugly face showed puzzlement. Evidently he had not seen Corcoran grabbing Wilson's shoulder.

Johnson asked: "You need me, boss?"

"No."

Johnson drew back. He seemed relieved.

Wilson spoke to Corcoran, still sitting. "Did you ever have a million bucks in your possession, all yours?"

Corcoran stared. His mouth became steady. What kind of a question was that?

He remembered Wilson breaking off a tense conversation to talk about Jean Benson. A queer look seeped into Corcoran's eyes. Was this man in his right mind?

"No. Why?"

"I have."

Wilson turned away. He didn't look back.

He remembered Jean Benson entering the cafe. He entered the same cafe. The dining room was empty.

He heard rustlings beyond the kitchen's swinging doors. He put his right hand on the counter.

He flexed his fingers. Relief touched him. His fingers were okay. He looked up as the kitchen's swinging doors opened.

Jean Benson entered. She carried a tray of glistening water glasses. He noticed quickly her hands had no rings.

She said: "Oh . . . . "

She put the glass-tray down on the counter. She looked at Matt Wilson. Matt Wilson looked at her.

Wilson said: "Your name is Jean? Jean Benson?"

"Yes. Who told you?"

"Corcoran. I'm Matt Wilson."

"Jim Wilson's brother?"

"I am."

She said: "Jim is dead."

Chapter Three

Matt Wilson looked at his skinned knuckles but didn't see them. Instead, he saw the long and muddy and winding Red River of old Texas.

He saw the Wilson ranch-house, the Smokestack Iron, hidden in spreading live oaks.

Run, Smoky, run! Slam your hoofs down fast and hard on red Texas soil! Don't let brother Jim's bronc catch us, smoky!

Jim's ridin' Waddy, a fast cayuse. Come on, Smoky, stretch out—leave Jim and Waddy eating red dust Texas!

Wilson looked up. "How long ago?"

"He was buried a week ago yesterday."

"Where?"

"Here in Sageville cemetery. My father and mother started this cafe years ago when Texas cattle came into Montana. I was the only child they had. I buried him next to my father."

Wilson had no words. He didn't trust his voice.

"Jim often talked about Matt Wilson, his brother, the world-traveling gambler. Jim adored you, Matt. He was so proud of you. Jim was only twenty-three."

"Three years younger than I am," Matt Wilson said.

Why did they talk about Jim's age? Jim didn't matter now. Jim—and Marie—both belonged to eternity.

"He asked me to marry him."

"Jim was a good man. Why didn't you?"

Idle talk? Or was it idle?

Wilson thought of the long and tiresome horseback ride from Great Falls into this Musselshell Basin. He'd taken Montana Stages to the Great Falls of the Missouri River from Butte, where he'd run a stud table in the Montana Mint Saloon.

Wild Butte, high-gambling Butte, biggest copper vein in the world, Butte. But why think of Butte, either?

"I wanted to love him, but it just wasn't there, Mr. Wilson."

"Matt, not Mr. Wilson."

She laughed shakily. "All right. Matt it is, then. And I'm Jean, Matt."

"Jean," Wilson said. He liked the name. It fitted her. "May I have a cup of coffee?"

"Certainly. Let's go into the kitchen. Hot there, but it's hot all over."

Wilson got to his feet. Jean snapped the front door lock shut. He followed her lovely back through the swinging doors.

He compared her with Marie. Both were the same height and build. All woman, both. But Marie had been dark, Latin; Jean was blonde, blue-eyed.

Matt Wilson caught his thoughts.

This woman affected him too strongly. Why? God knows he'd met more than his share of beautiful, provocative females in his life.

Singers, actresses, lady gamblers.

He remembered meeting Marie, that sultry night in Budapest. He'd been attracted to her instantly, and she to him. It had seemed only natural they would marry.

Was there such a thing as love at first sight?

Matt Wilson smiled. They entered a spotlessly clean kitchen with a huge cast-iron Kalamazoo stove. She seated him on a stool next to the open back door.

Flies fought to enter on the screen door.

She had a huge coffee pot on the back of the stove. She poured him a cup. "I've got a bottle hidden for some customers, Matt, who like a nip in their coffee. I never touch the stuff myself."

"I drink an occasional beer, nothing more, but thanks."

"When did you last eat?"

Wilson smiled. "About four this morning. A line-camp along a creek, where a lone cowpuncher was watching a bog hole. He shared his bacon and beans with me."

"Good heavens, you must be hungry. I've got a good beef stew in that big kettle there."

"It sure would be the thing," Wilson said.

She ladled the stew. "I tried to notify you, Matt. I sent a cowboy with a telegram to send you out of Great Falls. I sent it to the Montana Mint Saloon, in Butte."

"I had already left, Jean."

"We're isolated here. No telegraph wire, no rails." She spatuled french fries. "I didn't know just what to do."

"You did well, I would say."

Her blue eyes held tears. "Jim owned the Sageville Hardware Store—but you know that. It's three doors down the street. Behind the store is a big cottonwood tree."

Wilson ate. The stew was wonderful, the french fries done to perfection. He listened.

"Some evenings, after work, we'd sit there in a wide swung he made, and we'd drink beer and talk. He told me about your wife, Marie— and your baby that died—"

Wilson was silent.

"He told me how your wife died two years ago in Buenos Aires, and that the baby—a boy—lived but a few hours. It must have been hard to take, Matt."

Wilson said: "It wasn't easy."

"Jim waited so for you to come. He counted the days after getting your letter from Butte. He had a lot of the little boy in him, Jim did. That's why so many people loved him."

"Five long years since I saw him last."

Wilson stared out the open back door, but he did not see the alley dust. He saw a longhorn herd—sinuous, slowly-moving—coming into Cheyenne, heading north into Montana territory.

And Jim Wilson, dusty, booted, spurred, saying: "I'm headin' into Montana, Matt. I'm going into business. No more starvation wages for me, punchin' the other man's dogies. Why not forget the cards, and come along with me?"

"No can do, brother Jim."

"Went into the Maple Room in Dodge when we trailed through a few months back. Marie dealt faro there. She said she was lonesome for you, an' will be glad when you hook up with her this fall."

"I'll be glad to, brother."

"Wonderful girl. Man alive, she's a beauty. How come a woman that beautiful fell in love with a mug like yours?"

Wilson had smiled. "Wilson's luck, brother. Wilson's Man sits on my right shoulder."

"When you headin' south to Marie?"

"A week or so. Pickings are good here."

Jim Wilson went to his cowpony—tall, good-natured, grinning Jim. He swung into his Amarillo saddle. "See you aroun', brother Matt." He neckreined the strawberry roan around.

Then from his lips broke the yell—the rebel yell of the Lone Star State. Even the dogs broke out barking.

Jim hooked the roan high in the shoulders with his star-roweled Laredo spurs. The roan broke out bucking. Jim rode him with left hand high, hooking high ahead and behind.

The roan bucked around the corner and out of sight. Matt Wilson walked back into the Surcingle House and his stud table. Never again would he see his brother.

Wilson said softly: "Only one thing can kill sorrow, Jean—and that's the passage of time. When Jim was a small boy he had a siege of light rheumatic fever. Did he die of a heart attack?"

"No."

"What caused his death?"

Her blouse's front rose and fell to her deep breathing. With tears in her voice she said: "I wish you hadn't asked me that, Matt. I prayed you'd not ask me."

Wilson said: "If you don't tell me, somebody else will."

"The coroner's inquest— six men said it was suicide."

"Suicide!"

"Yes. Suicide."

Wilson shook a stunned head. "I can't believe that. Jim was the light-hearted, the gay one—me, I was the one with the dark savage thoughts. No, I can't believe that for a single moment."

Jean Benson's face showed anguish.

Wilson said quietly: "Please give me details, Jean. Where did he die? How did he die?"

"You remember the high rimrock ridge that runs across this entire basin, east and west?"

"I rode along its shadow for many, many miles."

"A year ago, Jim homesteaded below the rimrock about ten miles north. He ran in barbwire fences. He built a small stone house. He did the work himself, in his off hours."

Wilson waited.

"He ran a few head of cattle. He developed the creek running through the place. He put in alfalfa. Today it is green and high."

Wilson ate slowly, waiting.

"He spent all the time he could out there. His plan was to eventually move out there to live and ride into town to his store."

"Where has he lived?"

"Behind his store. He'd turn his bedroom there into a storeroom, he told me. Well, he was found dead in his ranch house."

"Wilson nodded.

"The door was locked from inside. He didn't show up at the store. I sent a man out to see if he was hurt or something. The man looked through the window. He saw what had happened."

Wilson lifted his coffee cup.

"The man you sent out—? He had nothing to do with the killing?"

"Definitely not. He was old and honest, an old Texan who came up with Circle Diamond years ago."

"You say *was*?"

"He was found dead in his bed three days ago. He was almost ninety, we learned—but he looked and acted younger. He was a good friend of Jim's. He loved Jim."

"The coroner's inquest?"

"The county held an inquest here in Sageville. I went to it. Jim's .45 had one empty shell. It lay on the bed by his right hand. His forehead bore powdermarks."

Wilson listened.

"The farmers gave Jim a big funeral."

"The farmers? Why?"

"He gave many of them credit—they needed barbwire, lumber, nails, such things. He wanted to see this basin settled. The railroad would then build in, Sageville would grow. He was very community minded."

"And Corcoran—? Corcoran was against this?"

"Naturally. When barbwire comes in, free range is gone. Corcoran is a proud man. He's tough. He'll fight to his death to hold what he had, what his father handed down to him."

"But he can't own all the land he runs cattle on," Matt Wilson pointed out. "Uncle Sam owns the public range. The land has to be homesteaded to get a clear deed."

"Corcoran knows that. He claims Squatter Rights, but we know that theory has been thrown out by courts all over. He's got cowboys filing on homesteads. When they get their deeds, they'll sell them to Corcoran cheap."

"An old, old story. I saw it happen in Texas as a kid.

Big cowmen fought nesters. The Wire-Cutter's War."

"Jim also located farmers on homesteads. He surveyed property lines, such things—established corner posts. A few months ago, the farmers showed their appreciation by electing him president of the Grangers, a job Jim worked hard at."

"Who took Jim's job as president?"

"The man Rand Johnson just killed, Mr. Horace Smith."

"You say Jim's door was locked from the inside. How did they get in to check on him?"

"The old Texan—the one who found him—broke a window, he said."

Wilson nodded. Things were adding up. Even if he'd not seen Rand Johnson murder Horace Smith, he'd still have been in trouble, because he was Jim's brother.

Wilson leaned back, his meal finished. He closed his eyes. He could do two things, he figured.

He could ride out. Or could he?

He remembered Bart Corcoran sitting in the dust, blood on his mouth. His own right fist had put Corcoran there. The entire town—Corcoran's town—had seen its boss downed by a stranger.

Corcoran had to kill him, Matt Wilson realized. If he tried to ride out, Corcoran's guns would cut him down. He'd inherit a sagebrush grave, unmarked, location known only by his killers.

Matt Wilson opened his eyes. Wilson's Man had not been sitting in his usual place on Wilson's shoulder when Wilson had stumbled onto that Smith murder.

Wilson then realized he would never have ridden out.

His brother had not committed suicide. He was sure of that. Matt Wilson knew he would have stayed and investigated.

Somebody rattled the front door.

25

Chapter Four

They went to the front. Wilson took a stool at the counter, coffee cup in hand. Jean unlocked the door. The customer was about twenty, Wilson judged—flat-bellied, not tall, not short. "Why was the door locked?"

Jean said curtly: "My business."

Wilson judged she didn't like the youth, who didn't appear attractive to Wilson, either. Tobacco-stained teeth, a blue chambray shirt, Levis, runover boots. A cowhand, plainly.

Wilson noticed the man packed two guns. He wore two criss-crossed, cartridge-laden gunbelts, his holsters thonged down.

His pale blue eyes appraised Wilson. Wilson met his gaze and read him for what he was—a young, foolish tough. Wilson did not discredit him a bit. Some of these would-be toughs could be very tough when occasion demanded. They were deceptive.

The youth slid onto a stool, adjusting his gunbelts to a more comfortable position. "A piece of pie, Jean. Lemon."

"No lemon."

"Okay, apple? Yes? Apple it is, then. An' a cup of java, too."

"Coming up."

Jean turned to go toward the kitchen. Her face showed displeasure. The two-gun man had spoken in a domineering voice.

As she passed Wilson she asked: "Something more for you, Matt?"

Wilson nodded. "Another cup of coffee, please."

"Okay"

The tough looked at Wilson. His eyes were narrowed. "I'm Ted Applegate," his thin lips said.

Wilson paid the tough no attention. Apparently he'd not heard.

"Applegate's the name," the man said louder. "Ted Applegate, mister."

"I heard you the first time," Wilson said.

"An' you're Wilson? Matt Wilson? Jim Wilson's brother?"

"You asked the question," Wilson said, "now you answer it."

Jean returned. Her tray carried a slice of apple pie and two cups of coffee. She set one cup in front of Wilson, then moved on to Applegate.

She looked tense, worried.

"Smart man," Applegate said.

"And you work for Bart Corcoran," Wilson said. "And he sent you over here, two guns and all, to size me up. That right?"

"You asked that question," Applegate said, "now you answer it."

Wilson said: "You stink, Applegate." He picked up his coffee and went to a booth, shoving back his coat as he sat down so his gun-handle would be close at hand and free.

Applegate's thin lips smirked, but he made no effort to follow Wilson, who sat watching him.

The door opened. An angular man, thin as a scarecrow, entered. He had buck teeth and a sunken jaw. His greasy vest sported a shiny tin badge.

He said: "Howdy, Miss Jean. Purty as ever this hot afternoon. How are you, Ted?"

"Jes' fine, Deputy McKay."

The lawman's weak eyes landed on Wilson. The runover old boots carried him across the floor to Wilson's booth. "Could I talk with you a while, Mr. Wilson?"

"Certainly, deputy."

"I'm Jack McKay."

"Glad to meet you. Sit opposite me, please. I'm keeping my eyes on that tin gunman at the counter."

Applegate heard. Applegate's eyes narrowed. He opened his mouth to speak, then closed it.

McKay glanced at Applegate.

Wilson said to McKay: "I take it Applegate works for Corcoran. And Corcoran sent him over either to pick trouble with me or size me up."

McKay blinked. "He works for Bart, yes—but as to the latter, I can't say yes or no."

Wilson quickly noticed that it was *Bart*, not *Corcoran*. He also figured that of all the local taxpayers, Corcoran, with his huge holdings, undoubtedly paid the most taxes in this area.

And McKay probably knew who paid his salary.

Applegate slid off the stool, pie consumed, coffee downed. He looked at Matt Wilson and left, the door swinging shut behind him. Wilson saw him pass the window, heading north.

"Corcoran's a powerful man around here," said McKay. "He owns quite a few town buildin's, not to mention his saloon—the Montana House."

Matt Wilson said: "I noticed the saloon. Only one in town, I'd judge."

"Only one, Mr. Wilson."

Wilson said: "What do you want to see me about?"

McKay breathed deeply, pointed chest rising and falling. "Well, you're Jim's brother—an' Jim committed suicide. I thought I'd bring you up to date on that tragic event."

"Begin, please."

McKay's story was the same as Jean's, except that the deputy skimmed quickly over Jim's relationship with the farmers. Wilson did not press this point.

"Could I ask what you figure on doin', Mr. Wilson?"

Wilson had expected this. "I'll stick around a few days. Jim left property. I'll tend to that. I'll probably sell it, as his only living kin. He's got a homestead, I understand—and then there's his hardware store."

"The store now belongs to Bart Corcoran."

Wilson's brows rose. He'd expected this, too. "How did Corcoran get hold of it so fast?"

"County tax assessor discovered an unpaid tax bill against it, so the county took it over—and Corcoran bought it lock, stock an' barrel."

"Tax bill?"

"Yeah, five years old. The bill wasn't ag'in your brother, but the former owner. He never paid it."

"Why wasn't he billed, and not Jim?"

"You can't bill a man who lives aways north of town," the deputy said, " 'cause north of town is the cemetary."

Wilson nodded. "I might pay that tax bill and get possession of the store deputy."

"That cain't be done, Mr. Wilson," the lawman hurriedly said. "Onct a tax sale has been made, the property is lost forever to the original holders or their heirs."

"How about my brother's homestead?"

"Bart Corcoran claims that, too."

Wilson said: "Mr. Corcoran works fast, doesn't he?"

"He's an aggressive man, Mr. Wilson. He's got one of his hands, Mel Griffin livin' on the place."

"And I suppose Jim's alfalfa fields have Bar Six cattle—Corcoran cattle—eating them down?"

"I reckon so."

"What about Smith, the dead man?"

McKay got to his feet. "You're a stranger here, Wilson. So what ice does it cut to you about Horace Smith?"

Wilson shrugged. "Usually such cases need a coroner's inquest. Witnesses are called. I thought I'd stay until the inquest is over. Surely I'd be called as a witness."

"Why?"

Wilson hid his smile. There it was again. Had he or had he not seen Rand Johnson cold-bloodedly murder Horace Smith?

"Just figured so," Wilson said.

McKay said: "There'll be no inquest. There'll be no testimony either way. The law gives me the power to decide whether or not a coroner should be involved. And I say, no coroner in this case."

"Why?"

"It's none of your business, but I'll tell you why—this was justifiable homicide. Johnson's word is as good as gold. Johnson says Smith pulled first. I believe Johnson. So into the legal records it goes: justifiable homicide."

Wilson nodded.

"So don't stay in Sageville on that account."

"You ordering me out of town?"

McKay shook his weasel-like head. "Jus' statin' a fact, Wilson."

"Corcoran ordered you to order me out of Sageville?"

Jean Benson listened, polishing the same water glass over and over again.

"You got me all wrong, gambler. Corcoran don't run me."

Wilson slid from the booth. He got to his feet, empty cup in hand. "High sagebrush surrounds this town, McKay. I rode through it on my way in. Higher than me and my horse."

McKay's pale eyes watched.

"I could leave town—but I'd not get far."

"I don't foller you," McKay said.

Wilson picked up his saucer. "You do, and you know damned well you do, tinstar. Corcoran himself—or one of his gundogs—would ambush me, night or day. And you know it—"

'That's between you and Corcoran," McKay said, "an' don't call me *tinstar*, remember?"

"I'll call you what I damned well want, and don't

forget it!"

McKay's hand was called. His pointed face paled, his lips trembled.But he backed off, just as Wilson had figured.

McKay said to Jean: "Frosty rooster," and then, hand on the doorknob, said: "Good day, Jean," and went outside, paying no further attention to Matt Wilson, who carried his cup and saucer to the counter.

"Corcoran's man," Wilson said.

"Ever since he first pinned on that star. And that was when I was a little girl. He's against you, Matt."

Wilson grinned. "He'll only do what Corcoran orders him to do. That goes for Rand Johnson, and this Applegate thing, also."

Matt Wilson unbuckled his gunbelt. He then rebuckled it over the outside of his coat so the gun handle would be close.

"How much the damages, Miss Jean?"

She shook her blonde head, "Jim's brother."

Wilson said: "That's okay, but you're in business to make money. I demand to pay."

She said: "You're just like Jim. He owed no man a cent. Twenty cents, Matt—if you insist."

"I insist."

He laid two dimes on the counter. He looked at her. She looked at him. He said quietly: "I'll see you again, Jean . . . and soon."

"Be careful, please."

Wilson tapped his right shoulder. "He sits there, all the time. Wilson's Man, Jean."

She frowned in puzzlement. He stepped outside onto the plank sidewalk, the sun hammering him.

While he'd been in the cafe, Sageville had come to life. Where had been empty hitchracks but an hour before were now occupied hitchracks with teams and saddlers tied there.

Downstreet, a group stood under the Merc's wooden awning. Matt Wilson judged them to be farmers from their clothing. He understood, Word of Horace Smith's killing had gone from farm to farm.

The farmers watched him from the block away. Wilson felt a wry distaste. He had little, if any use, for grangers. He'd seen them gobble up the Texas Panhandle.

It took no brains to farm. You plowed and disced and seeded and then sat back and watched the sky for rain clouds. If none came, you made no money. If any came and you had a crop, the middleman stole it for a few cents on the dollar.

Either way, in Wilson's consideration, the farmer lost. The soft-handed boys—the bankers, the commission men—stole his profit from him, and stole it legally.

He looked toward Corcoran's saloon. Rand Johnson and two others, gunhung also, stood under that wooden awning. Wilson ironically lifted his hand to Johnson.

Johnson did not return the gesture.

Deputy Sheriff Jack McKay stood directly across the dusty street, Ted Applegate with him. Applegate stepped forward, pausing at the plank sidewalk's ragged edge, and Ted Applegate said: "Call me a sonofabitch, Wilson."

Wilson stopped, a vacant lot behind him.

The town was silent except for a horse pawing at a hitch-post. Wilson noticed, from a corner of his eye, that the farmers were watching, and he caught the glint of sunlight on rifle barrels.

This burg was ready to fly apart.

Wilson said: "Do you need a reason, Applegate?"

Applegate gritted, "You son-of-a-bitchin' tinhorn!"

Wilson noticed that Deputy Sheriff Jack McKay had discreetly moved a hundred feet away from Ted Applegate. This was a put-up affair. Applegate had been sent by Corcoran.

Irony tugged Wilson. "McKay, there's trouble brewing here. You're the law, You should step in and stop it."

McKay hesitated, then called: "I see no trouble, gambler."

"Then your eyes are in the seat of your pants." Wil-

33

son spoke to Applegate. "Sooner or later, you'll force yourself to pull your gun. So why not do it now, Corcoran man!"

His words rang up and down the street.

Applegate went into his gunman's crouch. Both splayed hands went down, hit gun-butts. Both guns rose.

Wilson saw that Applegate was fast. He knew Applegate was faster than he was. He was no accomplished gunman. He'd practiced, yes—but he'd never shot a man before, let alone kill one.

Always his house man had stopped trouble at his tables. He'd seen his house men kill, but he'd never killed himself. He'd often wondered how he would feel if a man lifted a gun against him to kill him.

The time had arrived. A man now lifted not only one gun but two against him.

Matt Wilson flung himself forward. He landed belly-down in the dust. And as he went forward, he pulled his .45.

Dust rose up, met him. Twin flames belched from Ted Applegate's guns. Applegate shot from the hip. Dust geysered up at Wilson's right. Another dust geyser rose ten feet ahead.

Wilson hurriedly laid his piece across his forearm. He used a trick Wyatt Earp said he used: Put your forefinger along your gun's barrel—and point. He pointed at Applegate's heart.

His gun belched, kicked back.

Applegate took the lead in his narrow chest. It lifted him, drove him back. His guns exploded. Dust rose at his boots. For one moment, Ted Applegate, head down, guns sagging, seemed to hesitate.

Wilson held fire: gun still pointed.

Another shot was not needed. For suddenly Ted Applegate's knees folded, his weight falling. Applegate toppled forward on his face. He didn't move. His guns lay beside him.

Wilson swung his weapon to cover Rand Johnson and

the other two in front of Corcoran's saloon, but none there made any effort to draw against him. Carefully, he got to his feet, aware that Jean Benson had come from her cafe and stood to his left, watching.

"Are you hurt, Matt?"

Wilson said: "Wilson's Man, Jean."

Wilson's Man? Your good luck charm?"

That's right."

A man came out of a frame building that had a faded legend: *Jefferson Myers, D.V.M.* He knelt beside the prone Ted Applegate. He put his ear against Applegate's back.

"Doctor Myers," Jean quietly informed. "A veterinarian, but the only doctor we have."

Matt Wilson reloaded his .45. His fingers trembled. He pouched the weapon, its chambers loaded.

The stout veterinarian looked up. He looked at the farmers, at Rand Johnson, at Deputy Sheriff McKay, then at Matt Wilson.

"He's dead," Doc Myers said.

Chapter Five

Matt Wilson crossed the street, boots losing polish against Montana dust, to stop in front of Deputy Sheriff Jack McKay.

"You could have stopped that, McKay."

Something akin to anger lighted the deputy's pale eyes, then died under the coldness of control.

McKay watched Wilson, but said nothing.

Wilson said: "Or did Corcoran order you to stay out of this, deputy?"

"I wear no man's collar."

The advancing farmers laughed. They hooted and called McKay obscenities. McKay glared at them, but said nothing.

Wilson said: "Where's your tongue, tinstar?"

"Don't push me, gambler."

Wilson said: "Get back, hoemen," and the farmers stopped. He noticed women among them. Women who also had short guns or rifles or shotguns in hand. This could turn into what the Latins called a *matanza*—the big kill.

Wilson glanced at the Corcoran saloon. Corcoran had come out. He stood with Rand Johnson and the other two. He carried a sawed-off double-barreled shotgun, Wilson noticed.

Wilson looked back at McKay. He gestured toward the dead man. "How will this go down in your so-called legal records, tinstar?"

"What d'you mean?"

"You know damn well what I mean! Will you call a coroner's jury? Or will you put it down as justifiable homicide, as you did when Johnson killed Horace Smith?"

"That's up to me," McKay said.

Corcoran had moved close, Rand Johnson at his right. The other Corcoran men remained in front of the Montana House.

Wilson looked at Corcoran. "You heard what I told this tinstar of yours didn't you?"

"I heard."

"What have you got to say?" Wilson demanded.

Corcoran shrugged heavy shoulders. Matt Wilson noticed that Corcoran's nose was swollen somewhat. "Not my business."

"Not your business? You never sent Applegate against me?"

Corcoran said: "Can you prove it?"

"The proof was in the act," Wilson said. "If that's the extent of your business here, then get out and go over to your stinking saloon where you belong."

"You talk big," Corcoran said.

Matt Wilson's .45 suddenly appeared in his hand. "This talks bigger," he said.

Corcoran studied the Colt. Not an iota of expression moved across his beefy jowls. He lifted his eyes to McKay. "This man pulled a gun on me, Jack. You're the law here. Your job is to arrest him for threatening one of your citizens."

McKay was caught in the cross currents. Indecision ran across his peaked face, and then he found his out. "Come with me, Wilson," he said. "To my office. We'll fix out my findings there."

McKay had taken himself off the hook.

Matt Wilson spoke to Doc Myers. "You come along, doctor. We'll need your signature on the death certificate."

38

"Got nothing interesting to do," the veterinarian said. "I've decided I'm not Buddha. I get tired of sitting looking at my navel."

A burly farmer said: "We'll go with you."

Wilson said: "We don't need you. Let's get one thing clear at the start. You farmers have your problems, I have mine. Both are miles apart. So you go your way. And I'll go mine."

"Your brother Jim—"

"My brother is not me, sir. I'm Matt Wilson. He was Jim Wilson. We're brothers, but different people."

"I understand."

"I hope I wasn't too rough," Wilson said.

"You weren't."

A woman said: "Mr. Wilson, when you're through with that worthless deputy sheriff, could I speak to you in private a minute or two?"

Wilson looked at her. He saw a small, middle-aged woman in a worn calico dress. A sunbonnet covered graying hair. The marks of extreme poverty were plain upon her. Her eyes were red, as though she'd been weeping. Wilson guessed immediately that she was Horace Smith's widow.

"Mrs. Smith?" he asked.

"Yes. Widow Smith, now."

Wilson looked at Bart Corcoran. Corcoran had been walking back to the shade of his saloon. Mrs. Smith's words stopped him. He turned and stood there, big and gross and tough, for a moment.

'I'll see you later, Mrs. Smith," Matt Wilson said.

"I'll wait, Mr. Winson." The widow spat in Corcoran's direction. "You filthy thing," she hissed.

Corcoran said: "Thanks for the compliment," and continued on. Wilson, the deputy and the veterinarian went to McKay's office, a small cubicle situated in a vacant lot.

The log cabin faced south. Despite the door being open, the interior was torrid. McKay threw his Stetson on the bunk and mopped his sweaty forehead with a dirty towel.

"Sit down somewhere, men," he said.

Doc Myers sat on the bunk. Matt Wilson took the only chair except the swivel chair behind the old rolltop desk, and McKay's skinny bottom soon occupied that.

Doc Myers said: "It was justifiable homicide, Jack. Applegate pulled first. He also got in the first shots."

"Don't rush me," said McKay.

He opened two drawers before he found his big corduroy-bound big ledger. He opened it and turned a few pages, then found the page he wanted. Wilson watched him and knew McKay was stalling to gather his thoughts.

Wilson heard a noise at the door. He looked out. The farmers stood on the plank sidewalk in a talkative, hustling group, eyes on the deputy's cabin.

"All they need is a leader," said Doc Meyers. "Then, if they had one, hell would really tear loose its hinges."

"Please," McKay pleaded. "I've got too much on my mind, now. And on my hands, too."

Wilson said: "You're supposed to represent the people, not Bart Corcoran. It appears to me, McKay, that you're slightly confused."

McKay's pale eyes studied the gambler. "Would you do me a favor, Wilson? Either drop dead in your boots, or get out of Sageville."

Wilson smiled. "I'm too healthy to die right now. And if I try to get out of town, Corcoran's hands will kill me—preferably from ambush. And I'm too young to die."

McKay smiled for the first time. "That point can be debated, Wilson." He spoke to Doc Myers. "You'll swear that Applegate's killin' was in self-defense?"

"I will, deputy McKay."

A voice in the doorway said: "And so will I."

Jean Benson stood there. Wilson again admired her blonde, open beauty, and again he thought of Marie.

Marie had said: "There's an old saying, and it goes like this—I'm not repeating it correctly, but it's some-

40

thing about that a man should not live alone. If the wife dies, he should get another. Would you repeat me, Matt?"

"Never."

"Never use the word never. Please. Why not?"

"You don't climb the same hill twice at the same time. After climbing the hill, you're at its top, and from then on, all directions are down. You know all the hill's idiosyncrasies. its weaknesses, its strengths."

"And you know those things about me?"

"Yes, to a degree."

She had smiled. "To a small degree, though. What man knows a woman?" And she paused, head bird-wise, and put a finger to her lips. "And what woman knows a man?" She answered that: "No woman. Matt, don't ever live alone, please. Your thoughts are too dangerous to yourself."

"I'll remember that."

And then she was gone . . . .

Now Matt Wilson looked at Jean Benson. He smiled at her. She smiled at him.

McKay said: "It was nice of you, Jean, but we really don't need another witness. Doc's signature is enough."

"I just wanted to make sure, " said Jean.

Wilson got to his boots. "Come in and sit down, Miss Benson. It was very thoughtful of you."

She said: "I thank you, Mr. Wilson. But if I'm not needed, I'd best get back and work on the supper menu. Good day, gentlemen."

She left.

McKay wrote in his ledger, pen scratching. Doc Myers stared moodily out the dirty window. Matt Wilson looked at his boots. Finally McKay looked up. He spoke to the veterinarian.

"They just called him Ted. Would I put down Ted Applegate or Theodore Applegate, doc?"

Doc Myers smiled. "Put down Theodore and after *Theodore* put *Ted* in brackets, McKay."

"Good idea." McKay continued writing. Finally he

turned the ledger and said: "That suit you, Wilson?"

Wilson crossed the room and read "Reads okay to me." He signed the ledger, and Doc Myers then read and signed. Wilson said: "I'm a free man, then?" and the deputy said: "Free, Wilson."

Wilson looked at the deputy. "You and I might be together more than you think, deputy."

"Why?" McKay asked.

Wilson said: "I'm riding tomorrow out to my brother's homestead. I'm not riding alone. Not with Corcoran and his gundogs sniffing on my backtrail, McKay."

"I don't foller you, Wilson."

"Maybe you'll ride with me?"

McKay thumbed a bottom lip. Doc Myers stared moodily again out the dirty window.

"I might be busy at that time," McKay said.

Wilson shook his head slowly. "You'll not be busy. I'm a citizen. Your job is to protect me."

"You're not a local citizen."

"I'm a U. S. citizen, though. And your oath was that you protect citizens and maintain the peace at all times."

Doc Meyers said, "Wilson's correct, McKay."

Wilson shot a glance at the veterinarian. Doc Myers seemed amused. He appeared to be having a hard time keeping a straight face.

Wilson also suppressed a smile. Once again he had McKay—both boots in the milk bucket.

"You mean you want me always to ride with you, Wilson?"

Wilson nodded. "With you along with me, there's less chance of Corcoran or one of his gundogs ambushing me."

"McKay studied Wilson. "Hell, he might ambush both—" He stopped. "Will you do me a favor, Wilson?"

"What is it?"

"I've got a hell of a headache. Will you drag your ass

out of here, please?"

"Your headache might get bigger."

Wilson left. Outside, farmers watched in a group. The Widow Smith came toward him.

"Mr. Wilson, please."

Chapter Six

They talked in Jean Benson's restaurant.

Wilson dreaded what lay ahead. He knew he would not tell her the truth. He'd not tell her that he'd seen Rand Johnson deliberately murder her husband.

He couldn't tell her the truth. If he did, this town—this range—would blow apart. Farmers would be enraged. They'd move openly against Bart Corcoran and his gunmen.

Wilson knew that the majority of the hoemen were married and had families. Common sense told him this. Also he remembered the farmers who had moved in on the Texas Panhandle.

Very few farmers were single. You needed a woman to cook and scrub and clean, and children to help in chores. A child, to a farmer, was a valuable item, an essential asset.

If he told that Horace Smith had been cold-bloodedly murdered by Rand Johnson, in the ensuing fight some of these fathers, these husbands, would be killed. That was only logical.

And it was far better that they remained with their families. One farmer killed was enough.

Jean Benson brought coffee and rolls. Mrs. Smith said: "I can't afford those, Miss Jean."

Jean said: "Please, Mrs. Smith, please."

The widow's eyes held tears. Wilson looked at the

45

door. A burly man was entering. He'd seen the man standing next to Corcoran. He said: "Just a moment, Mrs. Smith."

He uncoiled his length from the booth. He stopped the man, who glared up at him from under heavy brows. "You're a Corcoran man," Wilson said.

The small eyes narrowed. "Yeah, I ride for Six Bar."

Wilson shook his head. "You spend no time punching cattle. You're hired for your gun. What's your name?"

"What's my name to you?"

"I like to know the name of a man I might kill," Wilson said.

The eyes widened slightly. "I'm Walt Byron. I want no truck with you, gambler. I came in here to eat my supper."

Wilson spoke to Jean Benson. "Does he usually eat here?"

Jean laughed. "Only the second time he's been in this cafe since he rode in to sling a gun for Corcoran. And that was at least six months ago, Matt."

Wilson said: "Get out, Byron!"

Byron said: "This is a public place, gambler."

"You came in to try to hear what Mrs. Smith and I are going to say," Wilson said. "Now get out—or I throw you out!"

Byron said: "I'm not leavin', tinhorn."

This time, Wilson never used his fists, as he had on Corcoran. His gun-barrel did the dirty work. Byron's .45 was streaking from holster when Wilson's barrel landed on the gunman's head.

Byron's Stetson went flying. The barrel hit a glancing blow. Byron was stunned, but not out. Surprise flared across his beefy face. He dropped his .45. It hit the splintery floor with a thud.

Wilson twisted the dazed man. He got him to the door. His gun rose again crashing down on Byron's skull. Byron sagged. Wilson heaved. Byron hit the dirt, sliding across the plank sidewalk.

Wilson unloaded Byron's gun. He put the cartridges

in his pocket. He threw the gun into the dust, where it landed beside the unconscious gunman. Then he looked up-street toward the Montana House.

One man stood under the wooden awning. He was Rand Johnson. Wilson's voice came clearly across the distance.

"Where's Corcoran?"

Johnson had no reply.

Wilson said: "Tell him to come and pick up his gun-dog. Or why don't you do it, Johnson? Birds of a feather flock together, the old saying goes—and Byron seems to be one of the same yellow stripe you pack."

Johnson said: "There'll be a day, gambler."

Wilson nodded. "There always is that. You or I might not be here to see it, but a day will always dawn."

Wilson entered the cafe. He smiled and said to Jean Benson: "I'm driving away your customers."

"That type of customer I definitely do not want."

Wilson looked at her.

She said, simply, clearly: "Nobody can straddle the fence long, Matt. You either go this side or that—or you fall off."

"You?"

"With the farmers, the family men, the good men—the fathers, husbands. They are advancement." She smiled. "I sound like a railroad advertisement, don't I now?"

"You sound good."

Wilson sat beside Mrs. Smith, who said: "You are a man of violent moods, Mr. Wilson. It is good to see a fighter—one who stands for his rights. My husband—he was too meek, he took too much."

Wilson remained silent.

She said, without warning: "You saw my husband killed, Mr. Wilson?"

The crisis had come.

Wilson did not hesitate. "I did not see the gunfight, Mrs. Smith. I came around the corner too late. Your husband was already dead on the ground."

Her tear-reddened eyes searched his face. Finally she said: "I believe you are an honest man. I take your word, Mr. Wilson."

Jean Benson said: "Byron's getting on his feet, Matt. He's breaking his pistol to see if it has cartridges."

"Keep an eye on him, please."

Jean lifted a sawed-off double-barreled shotgun from below her cash box. She laid it on the counter. Byron was bound to see it through the window.

Wilson said: "Why do you pack that?"

"For moments such as this."

Wilson shook his head. "That's about the most deadly weapon made, outside of a cannon. I saw a man shot in two with one of those once, on the plains of Africa. Nairobi, Kenya, to be exact."

"So I've heard," the girl said.

Mrs. Smith got to her feet. "I thank you for the coffee and rolls, Miss Jean." Then, to Matt Wilson: "I thank you for your time. Perhaps you could help me on another matter?"

Wilson's brows rose.

"I have two girls. They are six and nine. I am worried about my only son, Mack. He's sixteen. He's very hot-headed. His father—his father meant so much to him."

Wilson nodded. Jean Benson listened.

"The girls—they always favored me. Most say a girl favors her father, but Nellie and Maude are exceptions, I guess. Mack favored his dad. To him his dad was the world—and beyond—"

"You fear Mack will do something rash?"

"Yes. He needs the advice of a level-headed man."

Wilson smiled. "Thanks for the compliment, Mrs. Smith, but i'm a stranger to your son."

"I well understand, sir. But he admires you. You knocked Bart Corcoran down. You're the only man outside of your brother who really stood up against Corcoran."

Wilson suddenly remembered his own turbulent

youth. Hot-headed, tough with fists—had a man murdered his father, he'd have buckled on his gun and ridden out, immediately.

To kill or be killed . . . .

"I'll talk to him, Mrs. Smith."

Wilson and the Widow Smith went out together, with Wilson saying over a shoulder: "I'll see you again, Jean," and the blonde girl nodding.

The long hot day was ending. Mrs. Smith said: "Mack is in town. Where will he see you, Mr. Wilson?"

"There's a hotel here?"

"Yes, the Montana Hotel. Down beyond Corcoran's saloon. Corcoran owns the hotel, too."

"I'll be there. A bed doesn't care who owns it or sleeps in it, but first I have to get my shaving kit and such from my saddle in the livery."

"Corcoran owns the livery, too."

Matt Wilson nodded. "I've heard of such one-man towns. Good day, Mrs. Smith."

"Good day, Mr. Wilson."

Wilson went to the town livery. He had to walk past the Montana House. Rand Johnson loafed in the wicker chair on the long porch. He watched Wilson pass, but he said nothing.

Bart Corcoran stood in one of the big windows. He regarded Wilson with a morose face marked by a swollen nose.

Wilson grinned ironically. He lifted his hand to Corcoran. Corcoran did not return the gesture. Wilson smiled. He continued on.

The barn smelled of bluejoint hay, manure and saddle leather. The old hostler sat in his cubicle reading a week-old county-seat newspaper.

Wilson stuck in his head. "Tell Corcoran there's no use going through my stuff on my saddle. And no use to split the skirts open. I've got all my money on my person."

The hostler said: "Brother, you do want to die, don't you?"

"But not right now," Wilson said, "and not in this stinking burg."

The hostler went back to his reading. Wilson went to his buckskin. The horse nickered and nuzzled his sleeve.

Wilson patted the bony nose. He'd bought the buckskin in Great Falls. The buckskin had proven to be a good tough trail horse. Wilson had not been on a bronc for some years until Great Falls.

The first night out his inner thighs had been raw from the saddle, despite his heavy leather Cheyenne chaps. This had amused him. He had really grown saddle-soft.

He remembered Texas and pounding leather on roundup eighteen hours a day, wearing out three saddle-broncs.

He hadn't neglected his body, though. Each day he'd gone through his exercise either in his hotel room or some local gymnasium. You had to keep the old body hard and tough, for fitness of the body made for a clear brain and nimble fingers.

Booze slowed you down, too. Therefore, he seldom drank. The other guy could booze all he wanted to, but the other guy was not Matt Wilson. Jim had had the same philosophy. So had their father, who now slept the big sleep under Texas soil.

Wilson untied the buckskin. He led him to the back and the water trough. The horse drank. Wilson led him back into his stall. The manger was filled with good bluejoint, but the buckskin had cleaned his oat bucket.

Wilson got the scoop. He went to the oat bin. He scooped and returned to the buckskin. He put the oats in the bucket. The buckskin began eating.

Wilson looked at the hostler. He had seen him scoop up extra oats. Wilson hollered: "Don't worry, friend. Bart Corcoran has a lot of money. He can stand it."

The head went down to the newspaper again.

Wilson went to his saddle, hanging from the ceiling by a rope. Other saddles so hung, too. He untied his bed-roll, two woolen Hudson's Bay blankets. His shaving kit and extra shirt and socks were enclosed with the roll.

They were in a small case. Wilson took the case free, rolled the blankets again, tied them to the back of the Hamley saddle he'd bought in Great Falls at the Ario Saddlery.

Carrying his kit, he left the barn, pausing at the cubicle to say: "I spoke too late. Corcoran or one of his thieves already opened my bedroll and has been in my case here."

"How do you know?"

"The blankets were folded differently. One snap on this little case isn't closed."

"How nice," the hostler said.

Wilson smiled. "You're too stupid to be sarcastic," he said. "Sarcasm belongs to the intelligent."

Outside he met young Mack Smith. The boy introduced himself, and fell into step beside Wilson.

He was tall, gangling, with a trace of whiskers that so far were just a fuzzy down, but Wilson liked his eyes and his manner. Wilson said: "Let's sit here and talk, Mack."

"You mean sit here—this is the saloon porch, Mr. Wilson."

"Good as any place. Public place, Mack. Mind moving over, Mr. Johnson? This bench can support three."

Rand Johnson got to his boots, face white with rage. Wilson studied him and Wilson's hand was hooked in his gunbelt ahead of his .45.

"You don't seem happy, Johnson," Wilson said.

From the corner of his eye, Matt Wilson also saw Bart Corcoran, standing still beside the window. He saw Corcoran lift his right hand slightly. Plainly, he signalled his gunman.

Johnson also saw the gesture. For one moment, Wilson expected Johnson to go for his gun, but he had read the signal wrong. Corcoran was signalling Johnson to enter the saloon.

Johnson did as his boss instructed.

Matt Wilson and Mack Smith sat down. Wilson did not relish what lay ahead. He knew all words would be futile, but he had promised the boy's mother.

He saw Johnson move close to Corcoran, and then both left the window. They went to Corcoran's office behind the saloon. Corcoran said: "He's a tough sonofabitch."

Johnson nodded. "Why'd you signal me in?"

Corcoran laughed. "You want to get killed, you fool? He can outdraw you any day of the week, and twice on Sunday!"

"I don't agree."

"If I'd left you there, you'd be dead as a plank now — like Ted Applegate. That wasn't the time . . . or the place."

"Hell, he showed me up in front of the whole town. He just shoved my ass off'n that bench, an' the whole town saw me back up an' eat crow."

"Maybe I gave you the wrong signal?" Bart Corcoran was sarcastic. "Maybe I should have let you commit suicide?"

Johnson wet his lower lip. "What's the answer?"

"He jus' disappears. Vanishes, that's all.

Johnson's big head nodded. "I'll kill him jus' like you killed his brother, huh?"

Corcoran said: "Not so damn' loud, Johnson. Walls have ears, the ol' sayin' goes. He jus' disappears. I can control McKay, but the sheriff down at the county seat—he counts votes. Just now there are gettin' to be more farmer votes here than there are Bar Six votes."

"He'll disappear," Johnson assured.

Chapter Seven

Next morning the day began gaining heat at eight, when Deputy Sheriff Jack McKay and Matt Wilson rode north toward Jim Wilson's farm, the slack-jawed lawman growling under his breath.

"You're makin' my life miserable, Wilson. More miserable than it's been since I was married."

"You aren't married now?"

"Naw, my wife quit me three years ago. Lucky, we never had no get. She jes' up an' departed with a drummer— one of them medicine man shows, buggy an' all."

Wilson smiled. "I see you took it hard."

"Damnedest best day in my forty-one years. I got drunk for three days, I was so happy, an' me—I can't stan' booze. That is, my stummick can't."

"You got company, deputy. I've got the same kind of entrails."

"I thought I'd die when I got off the jag, but it was worth it. You know, somethin' that happened last night back in town has got me stumped."

"What was that?"

"That Walt Byron feller. The one you knocked col' an' threw out of Jean's cafe?"

"What about him?"

"He was found in the alley behin' the hotel this mornin' by Sig Nelson when Sig went out aroun' five to get his milk cows. Sig has a kinda one-hoss dairy, you know."

"I didn't know," Wilson said.

McKay glanced at him. "Well, you know now, fer what it's worth. Well, Sig cuts through the alley—an' here's this Byron bucko, sittin' up, his head cut an' bleedin'—an' him not knowin' what happened to him, according to Byron an' Sig, both."

"You talk to Byron?"

"Yeah, I confabbed with him in the livery barn. Claimed he never had any idea what had happened. He didn't have much time to talk. He was busy saddlin'."

"Going out to Bar Six to ride range?"

"Bar Six, hell. He was gettin' outa town—an' for good, he said. I said maybe Bart Corcoran owed him wages."

"What'd he say then?"

"Said to hell with Corcoran. He was ridin' out an never comin' back. I saw him light out. Another thing I don't understand, gambler."

"What's that?"

"You had room 101, upstairs. You was the only person upstairs, the clerk reported. Nobody next door in 103, he said. Yet he went into 103 this mornin', an' the big washbasin was busted."

"What made that?"

"He didn't know, nor me neither. He claimed the washbasin was whole the day before when his wife— she's the maid— made up the room."

"Washbasins just don't break themselves," Wilson pointed out.

"That's what I told Jake, the clerk. Another thing— Byron was all skinned up. Aroun' his mug, his butt. I asked him how he got so skunned up. He tol' me to kiss where he sits down."

Wilson hid his smile. "I don't understand it. Why are you telling me?"

The deputy shrugged. "Jus' conversation."

They rode on with only the plop-plop of hoofbeats breakthe silence. A flock of sagehens flew out ahead.

54

They were as big as small turkeys, Wilson noticed. They'd be bad eating this time of the year. They'd be strong and brown of flesh from eating sage.

Young sagehens in their first summer made for good eating. They fed the first few months on wild berries and seeds. They ate sagebrush leaves only during winter when snow was deep.

"So one of my enemies left, huh, McKay?"

"One's gone."

Again, the plop-plop of hoofs. Wilson remembered sleeping on the floor in Room 103. Byron had walked in his stocking feet, carrying his boots. Wilson had deliberately left the door of Room 101 unlocked.

Byron had laid down his boots, drawn his .45, and stuck his head into the room. At that moment the heavy white crockery had descended. To Wilson's surprise, it had broken in his hands and it was at least an inch thick.

Wilson realized the washbasin had a crack in it. He had carefully collected its pieces, and returned them to the washstand in room 103.

He then had collected Walt Byron. He'd pulled on Byron's boots for him. Byron's feet had stunk. Byron needed to bathe more often.

Then carrying Byron overhead, he had gone to the back door and, with cold deliberation, had pitched the unconscious man off the porch, Byron's arms and legs flailing loosely.

Byron had crashed down into the alley on his back. Wilson had not gone down the back stairs to see if the two-story fall had killed Byron.

He hadn't cared if Byron was dead or alive. Byron had come to kill him, and he had outwitted Byron.

Wilson had slept until six in his room, a chair jacked under the doorknob. He had met no more interference.

"I can't foller you wherever you go, Wilson," Deputy Sheriff McKay said. "I got my office chores to do, you know."

"And they consist of you sleeping in that swivel chair with your boots on your desk, I suppose?"

"You don't treat me with due respect, Wilson. An' you treat the dignity of my office in the same rough way."

Wilson laughed. "Do both merit my respect?"

"I'd cotton to an explanation."

Wilson shrugged. "You aren't impartial. You favor Corcoran over the farmers. You aren't even a good politician."

"How come you say that?"

"Politicians are elected by votes. They favor the group that can give them the most votes."

The deputy nodded.

"So far, Corcoran and his gunmen—and cowpunchers—have had the most votes, but from what I was told the farmers will soon have the majority—for more farmers are on their way in, a a farmer told me."

"You got a point," McKay conceded. "You know, Jean Benson cottons to you."

"Why change the subject?"

"Well, for one thing—you had me cornered, gambler. She never has given but one man in Sageville a tumble afore you, an' that was your brother Jim."

"You imagine things," Wilson said. "You'll have to decide soon. Which way you going to jump?"

"I'm waitin'."

Wilson grinned. "I kind of like you, McKay. You're not much on the brainy side, but you have a sort of winning way about you—a guy feels sorry for you about like he'd feel for a lost dog."

McKay looked at him. "Thanks a lot," he said.

Wilson hid his smile.

They rode along a wagon road that McKay said eventually ended fifteen or so miles north in the yard of Bart Corcoran's Bar Six ranch.

"Hold up a minute," the deputy said.

They had ridden over the summit of a high hill. North and east stretched a wide valley. A creek meandered through cottonwoods, box elders and diamond willows, twisting its way across the basin, heading southeast.

"This is where the farmers are located," McKay said.

Wilson's buckskin rolled the cricket in his bit. Wilson sat saddle and looked at the scatteration of farm cabins below. Most were tarpaper shacks, black spots against the distance. Most had gray smoke trailing upward from stovepipe chimneys.

"Cookin'," McKay said. "Grubbin' up for a day's work behin' a plow, or diggin' irrigation ditches."

"Irrigation ditches?"

"Yeah, the same. Thet crick there is Doggone Crick. Runs water all the year, even in a dry year like this'n. Dam's goin' in up there." McKay stood on stirrups and pointed toward Six Bar, whose many buildings could be dimly seen against distance.

"Who's going to finance the dam?"

"Railroad company. Contracts are all drawn, they tell me—and work starts as soon as a hundred more farmers settle. Your brother Jim signed for the hoemen, Mr. Wilson."

"The dam'll be almost in Corcoran's front door, won't it?"

"Yeah, about a mile from Six Bar. Canyon there. Natural place for a dam. Your brother built a little coffer dam in Doggone. He diverted water onto his alfalfa. Grew like weeds. Jim worked hard. His body an'soul was in his store an' his farm."

"Where's Jim's farm?"

McKay pointed northeast. "Over there. Cain't see it because of thet hill. Look at the bobwire they've strung."

Shiny new barbwire glistened in the bright sunlight. Farmers had strung fences with diamond willow posts. The land below was laid out in green squares controlled by barbwire fences. Cattle grazed behind the barbs. Around each section ran a community road, as the Homestead laws demanded.

'Different than five years back," the deputy said. "No fences, no fields, no green then—only when it rained, an' this country don't have much rain."

"And Bar Six cattle," Wilson said.

"I don't know," Jack McKay said. "I really don't know."

"You don't know what?"

"I just don't know."

Wilson smiled. "You just don't know which side to take, McKay? I can tell you this. Nothing or nobody will hold back these farmers."

"What makes you say that?"

"I saw the same on the Texas Panhandle. Cowmen fought settlers. It went into rifles and short-guns and the dead, but the farmers won."

"The Wire Cutter's War, huh?"

"The same," Wilson said. He studied the wagon road ahead. It ran through high buckbrush, twisted along a coulee dense with cottonwoods and willows, then went over another hill into another area of high brush. "Let's ride the ridge, McKay."

"Why?"

"From a high area, you can see below you, that's why."

McKay grinned. "You should be a longrider, Wilson. I done heard thet the Wild Bunch—Kid Curry and Cassidy an' Sundance—always ride the high country, scoutin' out what danger lays below."

"One reason, maybe, why they've lived so long."

They rode a high, brush-screened trail. Now you could see Corcoran's Bar Six some four miles north. The ranch looked big—big ranch house, barns, haystacks, wide-flung pole corrals.

"There's your brother's homestead." McKay stood on stirrups, pointing slightly east of north.

Jim's farm was a mile away. Wilson's eyes narrowed. From this distance it looked as though his brother had duplicated, on a smaller scale, the old Texas Smokestack Iron buildings.

A stone house, a dogrun, a kitchen and bedding area tied on behind, the usual Texas style. Wilson looked west.

There towered the Highwood Mountains. Snow-covered peaks with ever-present glaciers fed ice-cold creeks and rivers. There was plenty of water year round. There grass grew knee-high to a tall bronc.

Wilson had recently read where Uncle Sam had thrown open forest areas for grazing at so much a head. Corcoran would show sense if he leased and ran cattle back in the high-grass area with its abundant water and shade for stock.

Suddenly Deputy Jack McKay stood on oxbow stirrups, staring down at the wagon road a quarter-mile below. "What the hell am I lookin' at, Wilson?"

"Same thing I am, I'd say."

"Could I use your field-glasses?"

Wilson untied his glasses from saddle-skirt. He handed them to the deputy, who centered them on the road below, dirty finger slowly turning the adjustment screw.

Finally, McKay lowered the glasses, handing them to Wilson. "By hell, Wilson, that's Walt Byron."

Wilson adjusted the glasses. "Settled behind a big boulder for protection, watching the trail coming out from Sageville—and nobody but my old friend, Walt Byron."

"He's got his rifle, Wilson."

McKay looked at Wilson. "He's layin' an ambush for you. What're you goin' to do?"

"Nothing, right now. I rode out to see my brother's farm. I didn't ride out hoping to meet Walt Byron."

"Thet bastard tol' me he was pullin' out for good I kinda suspect you bounced that washbasin off his skull, Wilson."

"Perish the thought, please."

"An' you threw him off the second story of the hotel into the alley."

"Never in my life," Wilson said.

McKay scratched his jaw. "Mebbe I oughta ride

down there. Mebbe some farmer might come along. Mebbe he might mistake the farmer for you, an' shoot him dead."

"Lots of maybes."

McKay settled back against cantle. "But I ain't got no proof. He'd claim he was restin'. Or still-huntin a deer. He ain't done nothin' illegal yet."

"That's right."

"Guess we ride on, Wilson."

They rode on. Four hours later they rode into Sageville, and drew rein in front of Corcoran's Montana House. Each led a saddled horse.

McKay led a grey mare. Wilson lead a blue roan gelding. McKay's grey had a young cowpuncher tied by his hands to the saddle-horn.

Wilson's roan had a dead man jack-knifed across leather, hands and feet tied to the cinch to keep him from sliding off.

Rand Johnson sat alone on the saloon's long porch, reading an old copy of the *Fergus County Rancher*. He laid down the newspaper and stared, riveted to the bench.

Wilson spoke to Johnson. "Where's your boss?"

"Corcoran?"

"Who else?"

Johnson studied the man tied to the saddle-horn. The man was bloody, shirt torn—he rode head down, beaten, scared.

"That's Mel Griffin," Johnson said, getting to his feet. "He runs your brother's farm."

"Not any more," Wilson said.

Carrying his newspaper, Johnson moved sidewise so he could better see the dead man's face. "That's Walt Byron. Is he dead?"

"Dead as he'll ever be. Now get Corcoran."

"I'll get him."

Johnson hurried into the Montana House.

Chapter Eight

Bart Corcoran's golden watch chain glistened in the noon sun. Matt Wilson watched the beefy, clean-shaven face. He decided that Corcoran evidently was a good poker player.

Corcoran's face showed no surprise. His dull eyes were emotionless. He studied the cowpuncher tied to the saddle-horn. His eyes moved over to the dead man.

Finally Corcoran looked up at Deputy Sheriff McKay. He seemingly did not know that Matt Wilson rode with the lawman.

"Who killed Byron?" he asked.

McKay said: "We don't know."

Wilson noticed a group of farmers riding around the corner of the Merc and entering Main Street. They had met a farmer out hunting his milk cow. Evidently he'd told other farmers about the dead man.

Corcoran looked at the farmers. His face showed an expression of disgust. He still did not apparently acknowledge Matt Wilson's presence, so Wilson deliberately said: "We found him dead on the trail. He's been shot once through the heart, once through the head."

Corcoran looked again at the dead man.

Wilson said: "We saw him set an ambush when we rode out to my brother's farm. When we rode back, he was dead in the wagon-road."

Corcoran still avoided Matt Wilson. He spoke to McKay. "You didn't kill him?"

Deputy McKay said: "We didn't kill him. It was like Mr. Wilson says. But he did set an ambush."

"And I figure you ordered him to set it," Wilson said.

Corcoran spoke again only to McKay. "Where did you find him?"

McKay told him.

"Why are you riding with this stranger?" Corcoran asked.

"He asked me to," McKay said. "He claimed I owed him pertection, an' he demanded I ride with him."

Corcoran nodded. "I'll speak more to you later, McKay." Then, to Rand Johnson: "You and Wolf cut him down and take him inside. Get the carpenter over here to measure him."

McKay said stiffly: "What'll you speak to me about, Corcoran? Why not say what you want here an' now?"

Corcoran studied the deputy. "Don't get too big for your pants, McKay. Just remember who pays your wages, man—and who got you this soft deputy sheriff job."

McKay said: "Don't rub me the wrong way, Bart."

A farmer said: "By Harry, the deputy's beginnin' to act like he's got testicles, men."

"About time," another farmer said.

Wilson looked at the farmers. He saw young Mack Smith rode with the group. Mack's mount was an old plowhorse with collar-sore markings of white. The youth rode an old McClellan army saddle.

A lever-action Marlin rifle was tied to the saddle's back strings. Wilson judged it to be a .32-40 caliber. His eyes met those of the youngster. Mack Smith looked away.

Wilson remembered talking to the youth here on the saloon's porch. He'd accomplished not a thing. The youth had listened respectfully, but his eyes had wandered here and there.

Plainly, he been merely courteous, nothing more.

Corcoran looked at the man tied to the saddle-horn. "What the hell happened to you, Griffin?"

"Wilson beat me up. He said I had no right to sit it out on his brother's farm."

Anger reddened Bart Corcoran's jowls. "You had your weapons, didn't you? Your hand-gun—your rifle."

"I pulled against him, but he beat me."

"You hired on as a gun—" Corcoran caught his words in time. "You've bragged about how fast you were with a shortgun."

"Wilson is faster," Griffin said.

Matt Wilson said: "I pistol-whipped him, Corcoran. I tore down that big sign you put up, saying you now owned my brother's farm. I've been told on good authority that my brother faithfully filled out his homestead obligations."

Corcoran looked at Matt Wilson.

"Under Abe Lincoln's Homestead laws a man who files on a homestead has to live on it fourteen months and improve it by planting crops. According to what I've heard, my brother fulfilled all obligations, and Uncle Sam gave him a deed to his homestead."

"Where's the deed now?" Corcoran demanded.

A woman's voice said: "I have it, Mr. Corcoran. Jim suspected something might happen to him. He gave it to me to keep for him."

For the first time, Matt Wilson noticed Jean Benson in the group. His eyes met hers. She smiled at him. Matt Wilson nodded and let his eyes run over the others.

He judged everybody in Sageville was crowded around them, except babies in cribs. Boys and girls stood on the outskirts of the group, watching with big eyes.

"My lawyer says different," Corcoran said.

"Where is your lawyer?" Wilson asked.

"Down in the county seat."

"What's his name?"

Corcoran hesitated. "Myron C. Wheeler."

Wilson spoke to Deputy McKay. "There's a U. S.

land commissioner in the county seat, I suppose?"

"There is," McKay said. He gave the commissioner's name.

Jean Benson said: "Jim acted as land commissioner here in Sageville, Matt. I have his seal and government papers."

Bart Corcoran glared at Jean, who smiled at him sarcastically. Corcoran whipped his eyes back to Matt Wilson, for Wilson's next words had strong effect on the saloon man.

"Who's operating my brother's store, Corcoran?"

Corcoran wet his bottom lip and then said: "Oliver Moe."

"Mr. Moe in this group?" Wilson asked.

"Here he is," Jean said.

Corcoran looked at Jean. He said: "You're getting to be a public nuisance, Miss Benson."

Jean had no reply. Matt Wilson appraised Oliver Moe. He judged the heavy-set, burly man to be about thirty. Moe was heavy-handed, flat of belly, and he wore his six-shooter low, professional gunslinger style.

The Colt .45 rested in a halfbreed holster. Matt Wilson hadn't seen a halfbreed holster for a long time.

A halfbreed holster had an open end. The pistol's barrel stuck out naked about an inch. The holster had a rivet that joined it to Oliver Moe's gunbelt.

You didn't draw with a halfbreed. You slapped down, leveled, let fall—shooting from the hip.

Matt Wilson said: "You don't look like a storekeeper to me, Moe. You look more like a hired gun. Corcoran's hired gun."

Oliver Moe's eyes had pulled down. His right hand rode on the bone-handle of his .45.

"Who gave you the right to take over my brother's property?"

Moe said nothing. Suddenly he flew backwards, Arms flailing, through the crowd, the farmers and townspeople scattering.

Matt Wilson had kicked him in the jaw. Moe had flung

64

up his forearms—too late. Wilson was instantly out of saddle. Short-gun raised, he followed Oliver Moe, face savage.

Moe landed sitting down. Wilson's .45 chopped down, barrel smashing skull. Moe went over backwards. He lay motionless with a bleeding head.

Wilson whirled, gun covering Corcoran, who had been taken completely by surprise. "Did you put Moe in Jim's hardware?" he asked roughly.

Corcoran stared at Matt Wilson's Colt. Finally he said: "That's for me to know, Wilson, and for you to guess."

"Get him out, Corcoran—or I'll kill him!"

The farmers cheered. Matt Wilson stabbed them a glance, then paid them no more attention. Wilson noticed that young Mack Smith had his rifle untied. The Marlin covered Corcoran.

"He make a move, Mr. Wilson, an' I'll gutshoot him!" the youth gritted. His face was pale and determined.

"It's your rifle, boy," Wilson said.

Bart Corcoran spoke to Mack Smith. "Don't get too wide for your pants, boy," and then to the assemblage: "I've been fair and honest with you people, but my patience is wearin' thin."

The hoemen hooted him. Corcoran's jowls reddened even more. He looked at Matt Wilson, eyes holding glaring hate. "Before you came, they'd be afraid to ridicule me in public."

Wilson said: "I'm to blame, huh?"

"You are. An' you'll pay."

"How? In what manner?"

"That's for me to decide, Wilson."

Corcoran turned his bulk. He stalked into his saloon. Wilson grabbed Oliver Moe by the hair. He lifted the man to his feet. Moe was coming to, spitting blood, cursing.

Wilson turned the man. He kicked him solidly in the seat of his pants. Moe lurched ahead, then stumbled, fell. Wilson lifted him again by his hair. Again he kicked.

This time Moe stayed on his feet. He ran ahead of Wilson, with Matt Wilson following him, planting boot after boot. They came to the hardware store.

Oliver Moe tried to run past the door. Wilson's right arm snaked out, his fingers dug into Moe's collar; he jerked back hard, and Moe sailed backwards, landing on his rump on the splintery plank sidewalk.

"Corcoran will kill me," Oliver Moe gasped.

"If he don't, I will. Where are the keys?"

"In my right pocket."

"You still pack your gun, " Wilson said. "It would please me if you swung that holster up and made a fight of this."

Moe pulled a lopsided grin to his lips. "It wouldn't please me a damn' bit, Wilson. I'm a single man, thank god."

Wilson scowled. "What's marriage got to do with this?"

"I got no ties. I kin pack my duds in jus' a few minutes. I kin be out of this burg before you say Jack Robinson."

"You talk sense," Wilson said.

The farmers laughed. They jabbed each other in the ribs and grinned and whooped. Wilson snaked Moe's gun from the halfbreed holster. He unloaded it, tossed the six cartridges to a farmer, and restored the gun to leather.

"Now dig out your keys, Moe."

The store was bigger than Matt Wilson had expected. He was surprised at the variety of items it had for sale. Plows, harrows, discs, nails—Jim had carried a strong stock.

Moe lived in Jim's quarters behind the store. He threw duds—clean and dirty—into a canvas sack. He looked around. "That's all," he said. "All my life I've traveled light."

Wilson said: "Byron said he was quitting town,

too—but he stayed behind to ambush, and he's nail-dead now."

Moe grinned. "I'll profit by his example. Fact is, I've wanted out of this stinkin' burg for weeks now, but I didn't want to brace Corcoran. Thanks for cuttin' my chains, Wilson."

"You're welcome."

Moe left, sack over shoulder, whistling and grinning. Wilson spoke to Jean Benson. "Which farmer would you recommend for this store?"

"Mr. Halverson, Matt."

Halverson was a thin, scraggly-haired man of around fifty, who said he'd run a hardware store in his home town of Troy, Ohio. Matt handed him the keys. He and Jean went outside.

Young Mack Smith and Deputy Sheriff Jack McKay followed them out. Matt glanced up street toward the Montana house.

Oliver Moe was going toward the livery barn. He was opposite the Montana House on the other side of the street. He was directly in front of a building Matt Wilson had noticed was empty.

Two shots rang out.

Oliver Moe stopped. He grabbed his belly. Another shot roared from the abandoned building.

Moe turned, staggered, then went down head lopping over the outer edge of the plank sidewalk.

Matt Wilson noticed immediately that nobody was on the Montana House's porch. The three shots had come from the doorway of the abandoned building.

"I'll take the front," McKay hollered, "an' you take the back, Wilson."

Matt Wilson ran into the alley, gun in hand. The alley was empty of humanity. He sprinted toward the buildin's back door. He burst inside at the same moment Deputy McKay pantingly entered the front door.

"You see anybody, Wilson?"

"Not a soul, lawman. You? He sure made a quick getaway."

"He sure did," McKay puffed.

The farmers burst in. "There's a cellar door," one said. "Maybe he's hidin' down below."

One pulled up the heavy door. There was an old newspaper flared, and a few of the bravest put their hands into the cellar hole.

"He ain't down there," one said.

"Maybe he was hidin' on the roof," another said.

Mack Smith came in the back door, Marlin in hand. "I've already looked on the roof. I stood on a garbage can. Nobody there."

Wilson opened the side door. Directly opposite was a door to the Mercantile. "Who owns the Merc?"

"Bart Corcoran," a man said.

Doc Myers grinned. He winked at Matt Wilson. He was rather drunk. "That explains a lot."

Wilson nodded. The ambusher could have run across the vacant lot and entered the Merc without being seen from the street or alley by him or the farmers.

The ambusher could be hiding in the Merc or its warehouse tied on behind the general store. Or he could have gone out another side door and disappeared. Corcoran still owned guns.

Matt Wilson looked across the street to the Montana House. Corcoran now sat on the long wooden bench. Rand Johnson lounged shoulder against the wall at Corcoran's right, another hired gun on his left.

"Now who the hell killed him?" Corcoran asked.

"I wonder," Matt Wilson said. "I wonder."

Chapter Nine

Next morning Wilson was eating breakfast in Jean Benson's cafe when Jean slid into the booth opposite him.

Wilson speared a piece of ham. "Wonderful breakfast," he said. "You're a good cook."

"I try to be."

All other customers had eaten and left. Wilson and Jean were alone. She'd just finished a long conversation with a heavy-set townswoman at the cash box end of the counter.

"That lady was Mrs. Volvat," she said. "She wants to buy my restaurant and my house."

Wilson's brows lifted. "You figure on leaving Sageville?"

"I've planned so for some time. A couple of years, anyway, but up to now, nobody seemed interesting in buying me out."

"May I ask who is Mrs. Volvat?"

"She's a farmer's wife. Her children are all grown and back ease. Her husband worked in a Cleveland factory and they saved money. The Volvats, I would say, are one of the few farmer families with a little money."

"And she doesn't trust farming, I take it?"

"She has little faith in their making a living from their homestead."

"Water is the answer. Look at Jim's alfalfa field. All

69

the land around it is barren and lifeless, and his alfalfa is knee-high, because he got irrigation water on it."

"But Jim built a little coffer-dam, not the big dam they plan. Even at that, Corcoran—or one of his hands—tore out Jim's dam three or four times, Jim told me."

Wilson nodded. "Be some time until the big dam is built so they all have water. Doc Myers tells me the railroad company won't put in the dam until about a hundred or more farmers take up homesteads."

"And then maybe the railroad will go back on its promise. Yes, I know it's written into a contract—but railroads haven't a reputation for honesty, you know."

"They sure are liars in some cases." Wilson studied her over his coffee-cup's rim. Her blonde hair was immaculate, her skin clear, her eyes deep blue at this time in the morning.

He remembered Marie sitting opposite him at his always-late breakfast, for a man who worked nights had to sleep late days. Dark-skinned, dark of eyes, her dressing gown tight around her thin waist—

Wilson looked out the sparklingly-clean front window. This Montana girl—this light-haired beauty—was just as lovely, as appealing. He then remembered Marie's temper spasms.

They had made him downhearted. He had long ago learned that temper and life would not mix. You lived life evenly, as calmly as possible—in this manner, you got more out of life.

You didn't live long, he knew. You could live to be ninety and you'd still be dying young, in your own estimation.

He asked: "Do you anger easily?"

Her blue eyes studied him surprised. "Why, no, I don't. Anger is a waste of time, Matt. It repairs or constructs nothing. Why did you ask?"

Wilson shrugged. "Just a question."

"I used to have a temper as a girl. My father talked me out of it. He told me to be angry about man's injustice, man's terrible treatment of his fellow men—and let

70

small things take care of themselves."

Wilson listened.

"And he also told me that you could do nothing about such treatment, that it had gone on since Cain and Abel fought—so when you view life from his viewpoint, anger is a complete waste of time and ability."

"Well said, Jean."

"Are you angry at Bart Corcoran?"

Wilson considered that for a moment. "No, I can't say I am. He's tried to kill me. That puts it down to self-preservation, and that is a natural thing. He is mal-treating others, namely the farmers—but that is the business of the law not of Matt Wilson."

"How do you feel toward him?"

Wilson got to his feet. "Actually, I do believe I feel a little sorry for him. His way out is so easy. Just work with the farmers, not against them. But there's money involved. Without range, a big cowman can't exist—without free range, that is."

She went behind the counter. Wilson admired her back. He dug out his wallet and said: "The damages?"

"Twenty-five cents."

Wilson went to the door, then turned, returned. He said, simply, forcibly "I like you, Jean. You know that. I think you like me."

Her calm eyes met his. "I like you, Matt. And I hope you like me." She laughed a trifle shakily.

"This decision to sell—? My coming here never in any way influenced you that direction?"

She shook her head. "I told you I'd been thinking of it for some time, Matt."

Matt said: I'm a gambler. If I may say so, I'm a big-time gambler—Rio, Hong Kong, Havana, Paris, Rome, Nairobi. I'm a drifter. I have to be. When our baby came, Marie and I were going to settle down."

"Jim told me, Matt."

"Well, you know what happened— you can't be on the move and educate and correctly rear a child. You—"

He hesitated, plainly uncertain. She had running

71

laughter in her blue eyes. He saw this and he looked out the window. Nobody passed on the street. He put his arm around her slender waist.

He pulled her luxurious womanhood to him. He felt the rise and push of her splendid body. He kissed her on the lips.

She did not return his kiss.

His arms dropped. He stepped back. For once he had obeyed passion and desire, not cold logic. He was slightly angry with himself.

He said: "Well?"

"Well, what, Matt?"

"I guess I acted too prematurely."

She laughed. "You did, huh? Without warning, her soft arms encircled his neck. Her hand behind his head pushed down. She rose on tiptoe because of his tallness.

Her lips were warm. They clung to his for a long happy second. Then she settled back, arms falling. "Maybe I acted too prematurely?"

A voice from the doorway said: "I think all is in order, Jean and Matt."

They whirled. Doc Myers stood there. He weaved slightly in his boots. He carried a small black grip.

Jean said: "Doc!"

Doc Myers bowed from the waist. "I had no desire to snoop. I am not the snooping kind, as you well know, Jean Benson. But Mr. Wilson here and I were going to the county seat on today's stage—and said stage is soon due to depart, and with Mr. Wilson not in attendance—well, I went in search of the gentleman."

"And you found him," Matt said, smilingly.

"And in what I would consider very enjoyable circumstances, Mr. Wilson. I congratulate you both, but the stage—

Jean smiled. "Get out, both of you bums!"

Thirty-odd miles to the county seat—dirty, dust-filled, swaying miles, Concord thorough-braces rocking, swaying, the skinner wheeling and whipping and driving us as though Apache chased.

Wilson said: "He carry gold or something. Doc, to drive this wild and fast and crazy?"

He's a married man, Matt."

"Married man? What's that got to do with his driving?"

"His wife is back in Sageville. He is escaping."

"You need another drink," Wilson said.

"That I do. Thanks for reminding me."

They changed to four fresh horses at Halfway House, where Doc Myers bought another bottle and Matt Wilson a glass of cold lemonade, and then the ordeal began again—wilder this time, if it were possible.

The Concord skidded to a dust-raising stop in front of the Fergus County Hotel, all four wheels brake-locked, all four horses pulled back on their haunches.

Other passengers dismounted, the two women complaining about dust and rough treatment. One man—evidently a husband—challenged the driver to fisticuffs, and the driver started down only to step into the arms of a deputy sheriff, who controlled him by a hammerlock.

"Get out of sight, folks, please. Each shift he goes off like this and wants to kill the world."

"Turn him loose," the challenger said. "I'll clean his clock."

"An' both of you'll go to jail," the deputy assured. "Disturbin' the peace, assault and battery."

The wife pulled her husband away. Doc Myers said to Matt: "You fight him, Wilson."

"You fight him," Matt said, grinning.

"You've whipped about every able-bodied man in Sageville," the veterinarian said.

"You're not helping my cause, Doc." Matt Wilson spoke to the deputy. "Is your boss —the sheriff—in his office?"

"He was a few minutes ago when I left the office. I always meet this stage. Somebody's always callin' Joe's hand."

"Where's the courthouse?" Wilson asked.

Doc Myers hooked his arm in Matt Wilson's. "I know this burg. I'll lead you to it. Good day, Mike."

"Louis is the name," the deputy corrected.

Sheriff Hanford turned out to be a fifty-year-old individual dressed in complete khaki who wore a wide cartridge-filled gunbelt around his fat middle, a Colt .45 hanging on each wide hip. Matt Wilson had seen many such prototypes in Texas lawseats.

All had gone the way the political wind blew. When the wind shifted, they shifted accordingly. Votes elected them and they watched the voters, making a continual head count.

They were not intelligent. They were canny and political—oily and political—wise. They were born politicians—although minor ones. They had to be treated accordingly, Wilson knew.

They didn't wield much influence, because of their small political jobs, but when antagonized they could be singularly destructive.

They never forgot. They never forgave.

Wilson secretly wished he'd not taken Doc Myers with him. Doc was rather drunk, but rose to the circumstances.

Sheriff Hanford got laboriously on his boots. "Why, Doc Myers, himself. How are things in Sageville, friend?"

They shook hands, Doc Myers apparently stone sober. "Meet my friend Matt Wilson," Doc said.

The sheriff and Wilson shook hands. "Matt Wilson," the sheriff said, "I can't recall the name."

"New to Sageville," Doc Myers informed. "Jim Wilson's brother."

"Jim Wilson's brother! Glad to meet you, Matt. Sorry to hear about your brother's untimely—well, passing. Sit down, gentlemen. What can I do for you?"

Their conversation lasted over an hour. Matt Wilson discovered that besides being county sheriff Joseph Hanford was county coroner, county clerk and recorder, and his office also acted as county assessor.

Wilson realized that the combined salaries must have long ago made Hanford financially independent. He and Doc Myers talked it over that evening in their hotel room.

"You knew how to handle the oily bastard," Doc Myers said, "but he's slippery—and I don't know yet just how much he conceded to you, Matt."

Matt lay on his bed reading yesterday's *Great Falls Tribune*. "He's taking his time about deciding which side of the fence to jump off. Which will bring in the most votes—the cowmen or the nesters. Bart Corcoran or the Sageville farmers."

"He might finally jump—and land in mud," the veterinarian said.

Wilson studied him over the newspsper. "I see what you mean. The farming element might elect their own sheriff and put Hanford out of his ass."

"There's talk of that."

"What I know about this section can be put in a very small book," Matt Wilson said. "Could you help me out?"

"Well, farmers are coming in from all angles. They're settling in Judith Gap, the Highwoods, down along Flat Willow—even toward the Big Muddy. Corcoran isn't the only cowman with nester troubles."

"The other cowmen fighting them?"

"From what little I hear, yes. You'll notice that Hanford gave you no definite *yes* or *no* on any matter."

"I couldn't pin him down."

"He pretended he had little interest in Sageville, and he has turned all law matters there over to McKay. That's a lie. He's got his ear tuned in on Sageville. He knows right now how many farmers are located there, and what political power their votes have."

Wilson nodded.

"I think with a little talking—and effort—a man could go around this whole local stinking political mess. There are too young lawyers in town—just out of the university— yes, and other young people, too, who are

75

sick and tired of these old politicians."

Wilson shook his head. "I haven't got time. They may be sick and tired of these rotten *politicos*, but I'm sick and tired of this whole country. I came to visit, not to stay."

"Jean?"

"What do you mean, Doc?"

"Well, I saw what I saw. Hell, it's none of my damned business. Where's my bottle?"

Wilson grinned. "Over on the dresser."

Doc Myers drank. "I'm going out to visit some of my old drunk friends in the saloons," he said. "When I come back I come back."

"If you come back at all."

Wilson continued reading. Doc Myers' descending footsteps died against distance. Thoughts came between Wilson and the newspaper. Finally he laid it down on his chest.

He gazed at the ceiling, not seeing it. Instead, he saw a dusty alley miles south in dust-covered Sageville. One man had turned to untie his team. The other had shot him through the heart and killed him in his boots.

But it was not the fact a man was murdered that brought Matt Wilson to somber and deep thought. It was not that he'd been Horace Smith, and his assassin had been a hireling of Bart Corcoran named Rand Johnson.

Matt Wilson's attention centered on the bullet hole Johnson's pistol had made. It had made the same sized hole upon escaping as it had on entrance. Plainly it had been steel-jacketed. It had not been a soft-lead slug, for such a slug expanded as it passed through flesh. It made a much larger exit hole than entrance hole.

Wilson heard footsteps on the carpet runner outside. He tiptoed to the door, put his ear against the panel, and listened—but the steps moved down the hall and out of hearing range.

He jammed a chair under the doorknob, then returned to the bed—but not to his newspaper.

76

He and Jack McKay had scouted well at Jim's cabin. Jim had built a scaled-down replica of the old Red River ranch house. Hand-hewed wooden beams spanned the pine ceiling.

Dark concrete made the floor. Even the door was the same — two-by-eights, bolted hard together and stained. By instinct, Wilson had looked automatically toward the cabin's bureau.

And there the two oil paintings had been. Wilson had stared at them, for he'd not seen them for a long, long time. His heart had suddenly ached, and his throat had clogged.

"Oil paintin's," McKay had said.

"A wandering artist. Came by the Texas ranch. Jim had him paint them. My father and mother."

"Nice lookin' people, Wilson."

"Best in the world," Wilson had said. "Well, they're both long gone, now. It's a wonder this Corcoran scissorbill never destroyed them. Or Corcoran broken them up."

"A wonder it is."

Wilson had stood there — tall, handsome, tough, gun-hung — and had looked, the ache leaving. Two oil paintings, about eight inches wide, a foot high — one of a man with a close-cropped moustache and a blocky, good-natured face, the other of a woman.

She was dark, her cheeks thin, her eyes slightly sunken. She was the Slavic type, and from Sophia Wilson her son Matt had inherited his moodiness, his inclination for dark brooding thoughts.

Jim had taken after Jacob Wilson.

Wilson forgot time, forgot space, forgot McKay. He had moved forward, and his right hand had reverently gone out — his long thin hand, the forefinger out — and he traced his finger across his mother's dark sweet face, and he had felt the ache return.

As he stood there, then, he knew inner tears. He, so strong, almost broke, for memory crushed him. He stood there tracing the outline of his mother's face,

77

feeling the rough scale of the oil paint. His lips moved, but no words came. Then, reaching far into himself for strength, he regained his self-control.

And he knew then, as plainly as if his mother had whispered the truth to him, that his brother Jim had not committed suicide. He had been murdered. From his bed, he could have seen the two oil paintings, for they faced the bed.

And with them watching him, with the eyes of his mother upon him, with the eyes of this Texas pioneer cattleman studying him, neither Jim—nor any son on this earth—could have lifted a gun to his temple, blown out his brains. Not with his father and mother looking on.

Wilson had thought: "Suicide comes in the heavy dark, with no eyes to watch when the hammer falls."

He'd let his eyes roam around the cabin. There was nothing else he wanted. He took a blanket from the bed and wrapped the pictures in it. Then, with a last look, he went out the door into the land of dust and hate and rimrock killers, the two paintings under his arm.

He'd gone behind the cabin.

Above him, the dark and somber rimrock, consisting of black lava, had risen high and strong—a barrier plunged by geology across Mussellshell Basin.

The cabin had three back windows. The one allowing a clear view of the bed was broken, sharp shards clinging to the putty.

"They busted the window to get in," McKay said. "I was with them. He had the door locked from inside."

"Did the glass have a bullet hole in it?"

"A man couldn't tell. It was busted all to hell. I know what you're thinkin', Wilson. I looked for boot tracks in this lava dust, but they'd been there afore I got there, an' all was bootheels."

"He could have been sleeping with his back—or his face—toward the window." Matt Wilson had said. "And he could have been shot by an ambusher outside where we stand."

78

"I've thought of that, too."

"How did the wound look?"

"His head was blowed to smithereens.

"You look for the bullet?"

"There was a lead slug on the floor. Flattened out. No blood on it. He had a hole in the front and in the back."

"The slug could have been thrown there."

"Could have. I thought of that, too. I brought it up at the inquest. Doc Myers was dead drunk, as usual."

"He didn't look at Jim's wound?"

"He looked at nothin' but a bottle."

Next morning, Doc Myers and bottle, accompanied Matt Wilson, climbed on the Sageville stage to find Mrs. Horace Smith and her son, Mack, already on board.

Wilson was surprised to see them. There was but one stage every two days, and they'd not been on yesterday's Concord.

"Mr. Brejen drove over with his wagon," the widow said, "and Mack and I went along. Mr. Brejen is driving into Great Falls for a load of lumber. I talked to the sheriff.

"About Mr. Smith?" Wilson asked.

She nodded. "I got not even sympathy, Mr. Wilson."

Matt Wilson looked at young Mack Smith. The youth did not meet his eyes. He gazed out the window, eyes bitter. Wilson noticed he had a .45 strapped aroung his flat belly.

Wilson realized he'd received nothing, either, from Sheriff Hanford.

Young Mack Smith turned his head. He looked at Matt Wilson. "This is beyond the law," he said, "for Sageville has no law."

Wilson had no reply.

The youth tapped his holster. "This is the law now in Sageville," he said.

Matt Wilson looked at Doc Myers. Doc Myers' eyes showed nothing. He said nothing.

Wilson looked at Mrs. Smith. Her work-worn hands twisted a damp handkerchief. Her eyes were red.

79

Wilson said: "Boy, remember your mother, please."

Mack Smith's young eyes were agate-hard. "And forget my murdered father?" he demanded.

Wilson had no reply.

Chapter Ten

That night Bart Corcoran slept at his Bar Six. He awakened early, lying in bed a few moments, admiring the heavy cottonwood ceiling beams, the stained knotty-pine ceiling. Once again he told himself that his dead father had surely known how to build something that would withstand blizzard and scorching sun.

Once again he silently vowed that nothing—or nobody—would take Bar Six away from him, for family pride ran strong in the big man. His father had built this spread, tearing it from the bloody hands of the Assiniboine, the Sioux, and the Cheyennes.

Because he thought of his immense holdings, he thought of those who threatened to take it from him—the farmers.

The cowardly bastards . . . . they hadn't turned back the Sioux arrow, dodged the Crow battle-club, escaped the Cheyenne battle-wheel! No, when the land had become settled, the redskin stowed safely away on reservations, then the honyockers came in with plows and discs and seeders . . . and that cursed barbwire. Yes, and windmills, too!

He'd fight the pun'kin rollers. He'd fight till he either won or he was dead. His mind was made up on that. Sure, he could plant cowpokes on homesteads, but their rights—but the land he owned would be a peanut compared to the land he now ran Bar Six cattle over.

His mind was made up on that point. There'd actually never been any debate. He'd hold his ranch against the sodmen. Only one thing could make him change his mind on that point, and that was death.

He leaned over, silk pajama sleeve rusling. He tapped the bell sitting on the bedside table. It made a sharp, pleasant tinkle. He liked the sound. He liked the authority the bell gave him.

He'd driven out from Sageville in his buggy, one of the new girls sitting beside him, Rand Johnson riding guard ahead. The girl had spent most of the night with him until he'd ordered her to leave his bed so he could get some necessary sleep.

"Where will I go, boss? I don't know this house."

"Find a bed somewhere an' crawl into it, Angela."

"Maybe I'll sleep with Rand," she said coyly.

"Makes no never-mind to me."

He heard footsteps on the deep runner outside. The door opened, but Angela's red head did not enter. His mouth got a sour taste at the sight of homely Rand Johnson.

"Somethin', boss?"

"Where's the girl?"

"I don't know. I thought she was in bed with you."

"I kicked her out about three. Needed some sleep. She didn't crawl into your bunk?"

"Much to my sorrow, no," said Johnson. "She must've got into another bed somewhere. How many bedrooms are there in this house, anyway?"

"Plenty. Look for her."

Johnson returned in a few minutes. "She took a hoss from the barn an' rode back to town. The hostler helped her saddle."

"Well, I'll be damned. Send in the dquaw, huh?"

Johnson grinned. His ugly head disappeared. The squaw was young, and had recently gone to work for Bar Six as a housekeeper. She had wondered why she'd drawn such a fine salary—one hundred dollars a month. Within a few minutes, she understood why.

82

An hour later, she sat naked on the bed's edge, deciding it was better to return to the reservation, and hoping she didn't carry the seed of a halfbreed baby—for a halfbreed was accepted by neither whites nor reds.

"Cook my breakfast," Corcoran ordered.

The young squaw understood little English. She hesitated, debating the words, seeking their meaning—but Bart Corcoran gave her no time.

He swung his tough body around, doubled his knees and kicked her in the bare rump. Naked, she sailed off the bed, crashing into the wall. She said: "Oh . . . ."

She was instantly on her feet. She ran for the hairbrush on the dresser. Corcoran was on her immediately. By sheer force, he threw her out into the hall, and then heaved her clothes after her.

"Get off this ranch and stay off!"

Within a minute or two, Rand Johnson stuck in his head, Mel Griffin behind him. "What's the problem, Boss?"

"The squaw."

"She ran out the back into the hills. You run her off?"

"I ran her off. Can you cook?"

Johnson shrugged. "Eggs an' bacon, yes. Coffee too."

"Then get to cookin'."

Johnson and Griffin left. Corcoran dressed quickly. He was in a savage, bitter mood. The day had started out wrong. Completely wrong. He felt even worse after eading Johnson's breakfast.

"What the hell did you do to these eggs?"

"Fried 'em, of course."

"Hard as Doggone Crick's rocks. This coffee—it's so damn strong you can't dent it with a spoon!"

Mel Griffin snickered.

Corcoran glared at him. "You scissorbill gunhand! I staked out on that farm. Wilson beat the crap outa you. Even tied you to your saddle, paraded through town with you—draggin' me lower in everybody's estimation."

"I don't foller your logic, boss," Griffin said.

"I pay your wages. You work for me. You failed. Therefore it reflects back on my judgment."

"Roundabout way of thinkin'," Griffin said. "Wilson sneaked up behin' me."

"Why'd you let him do that?"

Griffin shrugged thin shoulders. "Man ain't got eyes in back of his haid," he said.

Johnson grinned. Corcoran turned angry eyes on Johnson. "You ain't standin' so high either, Johnson."

Anger touched Johnson's wide face. "If you refer to this grub I cooked, let me tell you, you never hired me to stand over a cookstove."

"Right you are," Corcoran gritted. "I hired you because of your gun. You claimed no man could outpull you. An' I still have to see you sling your pistol."

"Smith, that damn farmer. You don't see him walkin' around', do you?"

"No," Corcoran said, "but I see Matt Wilson."

John Johnson said: "Give me time, boss."

Corcoran snorted. He glanced up at Mel Griffin. Griffin's thin face was serious. Griffin's skull was beaten, skin cut. Doc Myers had taken twenty-two stitches in cuts made by Matt Wilson's pistol barrel.

For Wilson hadn't sneaked up on him. Wilson had openly demanded he pull his gun. Griffin had gleefully responded to the gambler's challenge.

Elation had spurred through him. His gun was clearing leather. His boss would be proud of him for eliminating Matt Wilson. Indeed, Corcoran might even give him a hundred-buck bonus.

Then all became a brutal blur.

For Wilson's gun came from nowhere, the barrel smashing across his skull. The blow had stunned him. Dimly he remembered dropping his own unfired gun.

Wilson had clubbed him unconscious.

"What's wrong with you, Griffin?" Corcoran demanded.

Griffin returned to the present. "Nothin'. Why ask,

boss?"

"Your face—you looked like you was goin' loco."

Griffin grinned. "Blame it on Johnson's cookin'," he said.

Corcoran got to his boots. He inspected his ranch, a delightful chore, with Johnson and Griffin close at hand. His bunkhouse was empty. His riders were either stationed at distant line-camps or checking water-holes.

He had a skeleton crew now, for this was the slack period between calf-roundup and beef-gather. He gained either way. Those cowpokes he laid off during summer months spent their wages in his Montana House.

When they went broke—which they invariably did—he gave them credit. Thus they worked roundups without being paid, for they worked off their credit-bill at his saloon.

His foreman—a gaunt, elderly Texas—was in his foreman's shack. Corcoran lounged on the bunk, talking cattle. Water was scarce. Farmers controlled almost all of Doggone Creek, principal water source on this southern edge of Bar Six.

Those damned farmers again.

"The crick's open only about a mile or so," the foreman reported. "All along its bank in other places are the barbwire fences."

Corcoran listened. He said nothing.

"Railroad says it'll build a dam in Doggone Canyon," the foreman pointed out.

"Ain't built yet," Corcoran said tersely. "Railroad lies. Lie after lie. Notorious liars. Promise everything to the farmers. Get them out and collect their freight money, an then the railroad forgets them. The railroad has got what it wants—their freight money out."

"Well, say the dam is built. If the railroad won't build it, the farmers might. Doggone will be dry below the dam. What do our cattle do then for water? We dig wells, maybe?"

Corcoran shook his head. "There'll be no fences by

85

then. This drought will drive them hoemen out."

'What if the drought breaks?"

"Their crops are gone for this year."

The foreman shook his gaunt head. "Some are re-plantin'. Rain come, an' any kind of a late fall—and some will have oats, at least."

"Rain ain't come yet. When it does, we worry then—not now."

The foreman shrugged. He wanted no part of this hoeman Bar Six trouble. Had Corcoran asked him to fight for Bar Six, he'd have quit his job.

He then remembered hearing about Oliver Moe's shooting. Oliver Moe had quit. Moe hadn't got to the livery barn for his horse.

"You're the boss, Bart," the foreman said.

"Don't forget it," Bart Corcoran said, and left.

He went to his horse barn. His mares were tied in the row of stalls, waiting to get in heat for the imported Morgan stud, now impatiently pawing in his corral behind the stable.

Each mare's oat bucket was filled. Mangers held good Montana bluejoint grass. Corcoran patted this mare, then that. His remuda was the finest string of saddle horses in central Montana Territory.

Montana cayuse and Morgan made a tough breed of horses that could stand long, gruelling circles come the hottest days or the most vicious blizzard. Bart Corcoran was proud of Bar Six's horseflesh.

He was also proud of Bar Six cattle. He'd shipped in expensive purebred Shorthorn and Hereford bulls. They'd bred his longhorn cows and thrown calves with more beef on them than their Texas mothers.

Only one point bothered him about his cattle. The calves still had horns. Not as long a horn as their mothers, but horns nonetheless.

Horn length had made no difference a few years ago when cattle were driven overland to the Chicago or St. Paul market, but now cattle were shipped in cattle cars since the railroads had inched west across the prairies, heading for the distant mountains and passage to the Pacific.

Without horns, a cowman could put more head in one cattle car. Therefore this cowpunchers dehorned all yearlings now. Although his imported bulls were polled, nevertheless most calves had horns.

He was surprised to see Sheriff Zachary Hanford wheel his ornate black-and-red buggy into the Bar Six yard at noon, a team of sparkling bay mares under harness, a black man handling the lines.

The buggy made a circle, dust rising under spinning wheels, then stopped in front of the yard-gate, team sweaty and nervous under stern ribbons.

Johnson, Griffin and Corcoran were eating dinner in the dining room. Corcoran saw the sheriff through the big front window.

"What t'hell brings him out in this heat?" Johnson wondered.

Griffin said: "The fat bastard finally got off his sitter for a while, it looks like."

Corcoran got to his feet. "Can the compliments, men. We got to act like we're glad to see him."

"Damned parasite," Johnson said.

Griffin said: "What county bigwig isn't?"

Corcoran snagged his Stetson from the hatrack and went outside, saying: "Sheriff Hanford. What a nice surprise. Light and eat a spell, friend. Hot day to drive in a buggy, even with a good top like yours has."

Hanford came down, polished boots hitting dust. He wore a yellow buckskin shirt, buckskin trousers and a buckskincolored Stetson. His gun swung on his fat right hip in a buckskin colored leather holster.

"Stable your team," Corcoran told the Negro. "Hostler will take over. Barn with the big white door. Then the cook will have some grub for you in the cookschack."

The buggy wheeled toward the barn. Corcoran took Hanford by the elbow. "Got some ice, and somethin' to wash aroun' it, sheriff."

"Hit the spot," Hanford said.

They entered the big ranch house, with Corcoran wondering, why this fat sonofabitch was out here in this hot weather. Johnson and Griffin had departed to ther rooms.

Corcoran seated the lawman in the biggest chair, then hurried to the kitchen for ice and Tom Jones. "Cook left me," he hollered back, "so we're on our own till we find another."

Hanford sipped. "Ah," he said, "ah."

Corcoran sat on the divan. "What brings you out here this distance in such heat?"

"Looking," Hanford said. "There's been trouble?"

Corcoran's brows rose. "Trouble? On this grass? Who told you such a fabrication, Sheriff Hanford?"

"A man named Wilson was in my office in the county seat two days ago. Asked a bunch of questions: Said he thought his brother had been murdered and things like that."

"A gambler who drifted in," Corcoran said. "A trouble maker. Came to visit his brother, he claims. I wish you'd have sat as coroner on that jury, sheriff. Then things wouldn't be so confused now. When you sit as coroner, the case comes out different."

Hanford showed appreciation. "Sorry, I guess I should have driven over to preside, but I always send a deputy out on these long distance—ain't as young as I was once, Corcoran."

"Who is?" Corcoran countered. "What about this Wilson?"

"He botherin' you?"

"Not particularly. There's always some troublemaker."

"He tole me he killed a man, Applegate. Killed him on one of Sageville's streets. Showed me the signature of Doc Myers an' Deputy McKay, making it self-defense. Who was this Applegate character?"

"Another drifter. Came into town right before Wilson. I think they'd had trouble before, somewhere before comin' to Sageville. They fought it out—and Wilson won."

The sheriff nodded. His eyes were lidded. Corcoran felt uneasy. So far he'd run this section of the county to suit him. McKay had been weak and pliable, just holding down his office seat and getting his monthly paycheck. But now McKay—

Everything had changed since Matt Wilson had ridden in, and not for the better.

"This farmer—what's his name? Oh yeah, Smith. How could I forget such a common name? Read where Smith was the most popular name in the U.S. He got killed?"

Corcoran summoned a puzzled face. "Damn nice guy, sheriff. President of the local Grange, he was. Jumped on a man named Johnson. Johnson killed him in self-defense. Deputy McKay has the death certificate, and he signed it as justifiable homicide, I understand."

"Johnson?" Sheriff Hanford rubbed his double-chin. "He the Rand Johnson who works for you?"

"You're right, sheriff. One of my cowpunchers. Him an' Smith has had bad blood between them for some time. Smith got drunk onct and called Johnson a sonofabitch, or somethin' like that."

"I can see Johnson's point of view. To call a man that is to imply his mother was a dog. What happened to Moe Oliver?"

Corcoran hesitated. Matt Wilson undoubtedly had really revealed all to the sheriff. Corcoran wished his lawyer were here, but Myron G. Wheeler was in the county seat, of course.

"Damned if I know, Sheriff. Man walked past an ol' buildin' in Sageville, somebody shot as him an' he dropped dead."

"Don't know who shot him?"

Corcoran shook his head. "Everybody ran fast to the buildin', but it was empty. Not even any empty ca'tridge cases layin' aroun'. Killer left no traces of nothin' behin'."

The sheriff nodded. "Lots of funerals lately in Sageville. I suppose McKay's workin' on these cases. What d'you think of Jack?"

"Good lawman."

Sheriff Hanford yawned. "Didn't get much sleep last night. Little grandson sick with colic. Got better toward mornin'. Mind if I catch a few winks in a bedroom?"

"Be glad to accommodate you, sheriff."

The lawman stood up. "Glad McKay's got everythin' under control in Sageville. I heard the farmers are goin' have a meetin' tonight in their schoolhouse. Guess I should, as a county official, attend, but first a little shuteye."

Corcoran showed the sheriff an empty bedroom. Hanford thanked him and entered, closing the door. Corcoran walked thoughtfully down the hall back to the living room.

He met Johnson and Griffin. "What makes that bastard come out this direction?" Johnson asked.

"I don't know," Corcoran said. "I hinted all aroun', but he asked more questions than me. He's goin' to the Granger meetin' tonight, he said."

Griffin's brows rose. Johnson flexed his knuckles. "Sonofabitch is out countin' votes," Johnson said.

Corcoran smiled. "I'll drive him over to the meetin'. I best attend it myself, I think."

"Why?" Johnson asked.

"Learn the enemy's plans," Bart Corcoran said.

Griffin's brows rose even higher.

Chapter Eleven

The Rochester buggy moved down the dusty lane, its sorrel team loafing against tugs, Matt Wilson handling the lines, Jean Benson sitting beside him. Dusk was creeping over Montana rangelands.

Wilson's blue eyes ran here, there. "Nice land if it had rain." He looked south. "That wheat field is gone. Farmer's plowing it under for fertilizer so all won't be lost."

"Good soil, Matt, and it needs only one thing—water."

"That's all they need in Hell, too," Wilson said.

"Yes, and good neighbors," Jean said.

Wilson scowled. He batted at mosquitoes. "Wish the wind would come up again. These mosquitoes are enogh to drive a man loco. I haven't been in this section long, but I've already noticed one thing."

"Yes!"

"The wind blows all the time except for a short period when the sun rises and sets, and then it dies for some reason."

"And millions of mosquitoes swarm out of nowhere," Jean said. "Range horses run to escape into the timber. A mosquito won't go in where it's dark, you know."

Wilson's scowl deepened. "I really shouldn't be going to this Grange meeting. The farmers might read my attendance wrong, and think I've decided to be on their side."

"I'll explain it to them," Jean said.

Wilson put his arm around her slender shoulders. She looked up at him. He kissed her. She kissed him. She squeezed his hand. "Matt . . . ." she quietly said. "Matt Wilson . . . ."

Wilson kissed her again. "I've made up my mind. I'm giving Jim's homestead —the house and everything in it to—Horace Smith's widow."

"I like that. And Jim's store?"

"The county never sold it to Corcoran. That was a false deal Corcoran and his shyster lawyer hatched up. I know, because I checked in the county seat. The store is mine through inheritance."

"What are you going to do with it?"

"The farmers are organizing a cooperative and buying it. The payments will go into the county seat bank. I've arranged that, too. After ten years the accumulated sum will go into building a co-op bank for the farmers here in Sageville."

"Who'll run the store?"

"Russel Halversen and Jack McKay."

"McKay? He's got a job."

"He's quitting the deputy's job. Had enough, he says."

"Does Corcoran know?"

"I don't know. How's the sale going on your house and cafe?"

"The Volvats will pay cash for both. I'm pricing each rather low to get rid of them fast. It'll be good to get away from Sageville. You know, I've never been any further away than Great Falls, and that's just a short distance."

"You've got lots of traveling ahead of you," Matt Wilson said.

"Matt, let me speak seriously, please. We've got all our finances wound up, or close to it."

"Yes."

92

"Matt, why don't we leave?"

Matt Wilson shook his head. "I'll leave when I know for sure how my brother died. I think he was murdered—shot through the window while sleeping in bed."

"But, Matt—"

"I know what worries you. It worries me, too. I don't want to die. But Jim was my brother—and I loved him. He had a long and good life ahead, and if an assassin's bullet cut his life short, whoever fired it is going to pay—or else I'm going to die."

"Revenge is an idle, insignificant thing, Matt."

Matt Wilson shook his head. "I can't agree with you. There is more than mere revenge in this. There is a thing called justice. A killer cannot be allowed to roam free to kill again. Justice is made to protect the innocent."

"I understand that, but—all right, I'll say it. What will I do if you are killed?"

"The answer is simple. You'll live until you die."

Jean Benson studied his serious face. "I know that. But it would be much nicer to live *with* you than *without* you."

Matt Wilson had been serious long enough. "How do you know?" he jokingly asked. "You've known me but a few days. Maybe I'll beat you and make you work outside so I can loaf around the house and drink beer and be a man."

"Oh, you're deliberately changing the subject. I wonder who shot and killed Oliver Moe."

"Corcoran or one of his gunhands."

"How are you going to prove Jim was murdered?"

"I am going to exhume his body."

He heard Jean gasp. "You mean—dig him up, Matt?"

"Definitely. Doc Myers says he can tell whether or not Jim was shot from behind or the front, and such things."

There was a quarter-mile of silence broken only by the sound of steel rims on dust and gravel and the plop-plop of horse-hooves. Finally Jean said, "Correct me if I am wrong, Matt."

"I'll listen, honey."

"You think Jim had his back to that window. The window was up and the curtain pulled to one side so air could get through, for the night was hot. And you think somebody shot in and hit Jim in the head?"

"That's what I think."

"What did he shoot? a handgun or a rifle?"

"A rifle."

"Why do you say a rifle?"

"I saw powder burns on the window-ledge. He laid his rifle on the ledge, took careful aim, and fired—but his rifle was slightly tilted to one side, and powder burned the wood slightly."

"You show this to anybody else?"

"Jack McKay and Doc Myers."

"What'd they sat?"

"Same as I said. Then, with a rifle bullet through Jim's brain, the killer swung into the room through the window. With a short-gun, he shot Jim in the head, so as to leave powder-burns that would say suicide."

"Jim's bed was against the end wall. The window is about one-third in from that wall on the back wall. The rifle's bullet would enter at an angle, the back entrance low on his skull, wouldn't it?"

"That's what I figure. I've investigated the coroner's inquest as much as possible. The sheriff didn't come over to act as coroner in person. He sent a deputy out to preside. That right?"

"Yes, Deputy Arnesen. Ernest Arnesen."

"And the jury didn't see the back of Jim's head?"

"No. He lay on his back. All of him was covered. Arnesen pulled the sheet down only to Jim's neck so all could see the powder-burns. But he had but one hole—a big one—in his forehead, Matt."

"There'd be only one in front, but two behind."

"I don't understand."

"Jim's dead. A pistol was placed over the hole where the rifle's bullet came out, in his forehead. The pistol was fired into that same hole. Naturally, it come out behind, above the rifle bullet."

Jean Benson shuddered despite the heavy prairie heat. "Then in the back of his skull would be two bullet holes? And in front, what appeared to be only one—and really was two?"

"That's the way I figure it. And the only way I can make sure is to exhume his body."

"But he's been dead—and buried—some days now."

Matt Wilson understood. "Yes, the body will be in bad shape, but Doc claims he can tell for sure—and I'll sure know whether or not there's one or two holes in the back of his skull."

"Did you get permission to exhume in the county seat? Surely one would have to get legal permission first, wouldn't he?"

"I asked Sheriff Hanford about it. He said for me to go ahead. He knows of no territorial statute dealing with a case like this. He even called in the county attorney for his verdict."

"County attorney? The country attorney is that shyster Myron Wheeler, and Wheeler is Corcoran's lawyer. Wheeler'll tell Corcoran what you plan to do, Matt!"

"Maybe that's what I wanted."

Jean shook her blonde head. "Another riddle, Matt—and no more, please."

"I *want* Bart Corcoran to worry. Maybe he personally killed Jim, maybe one of his gundogs did. But if Wheeler tells Corcoran, Corcoran will really worry."

"And he might act. Or order a beast like Johnson—or that Griffin rat—to act."

Matt Wilson smiled. "Then Corcoran would the same as admit his guilt before the whole world, wouldn't he?"

"I doubt if it would be read that way, Matt. Corcoran hates you. You killed his man Applegate. You knocked Corcoran down. You've ridiculed him by pistol-whipping Griffin. Corcoran has a handful of reasons for hitting at you, Matt."

"I got a few myself against Corcoran."

The rig topped a high summit. Matt pulled in the broncs to give them a breathing spell. Below lay the basin, stretching in all directions for miles and miles.

Doggone Creek meandered through the area of fenced fields and gray sagebrush. Farmers' hundred-and-sixty-acre homesteads were barren blotches carved out of grayness.

The setting sun reflected from brand-new recently-strung barbwire. Diamond willow and cottonwood posts were still green lumber, they'd been cut down so recently.

Cabins consisted of log shacks and brush wickiups. Sunlight also glinted off shacks made of corrugated sheet-iron. Matt Wilson shook his head slowly.

"I don't know," he said.

Jean Benson thoughtfully said: "It'll be a struggle, but they seem happy to accept the challenge—that is, if not for Corcoran and his Bar Six riders."

"Hard way to make a buck," Wilson said.

"I perhaps understand them better than you, Matt, because I've been around them since the day the first one came a year ago. The East is crowded. All they had there was slave labor in some manufacturing plant. Twelve and fourteen hours a day in the dim light, doing this, that—then home, a brief sleep, and back again."

"They call it civilization," Matt Said.

She glanced at him. "Did I detect cynicism in your voice? Anyway, here they may have less—and that is debatable—but they are their own bosses. If they want to take the afternoon off and fish, they can take the afternoon off and fish."

"Freedom of movement," Matt said, "but how about freedom from want?"

"They live more or less off the country. Deer, elk, antelope for meat; yes, and sagehen, grouse, prairie-chicken. Wild onions along the creek banks, a few spuds at home, some garden, that they carry water to from Doggone."

"Then all they need buy in line of grub is salt and

sugar."

"That, and clothing. Matt, look!"

Jean had grabbed up the rifle leaning beside her. Her rifle-barrel pointed northwest toward Bar Six.

Matt said: "Only a dust cloud."

"Riders, Matt. I glimpse them atop that far hill. Riders, coming from Bar Six!"

Matt held the team stationary. Within a few minutes, below them, Mel Griffin, riding hard, swept out of the brush, brandishing a Winchester, his horse stretched out, mane and tail flying.

Griffin roared over a hill, then high brush hid him, only dust betraying his passing. Two other riders now appeared, riding fast and viciously, hoofs scattering dust.

Sheriff Hanford rode on his stirrups, fat body bent forward, his blue roan gelding on a wild, deadly gallop and a pace behind the lawman thundered a midnight black stud, its rider solid and deep in Miles City saddle, his Winchester resting in saddle-boot.

"Bart Corcoran," Jean said.

"Yes, and Sheriff Hanford," Matt Said.

The lawman and rancher fell from sight, following Mel Griffin's fast hoofbeats. Still, a dust cloud persisted, and soon Rand Johnson, also brandishing a Winchester, came into view, his bay mare at a determined, mile-killing run.

The first three apparently had not seen the buggy and its occupants, but Rand Johnson noticed them.

His knotted reins dropped down on the bay's neck. The mare ran without guidance. Johnson threw his rifle in the air. He caught it with his left hand.

His free right hand drew his six-shooter. He fired twice into the air, slanting his bullets to the west.

Then he was gone.

Wilson's face was pale with anger. "I didn't hear his bullets sing," he finally said.

"He shot far overhead of us."

Wilson said: "A guard riding ahead, one behind. Now

97

why would the sheriff be riding with Corcoran?"

"They're old friends."

Wilson looked at the three retreating dust clouds. Four miles below was Doggone School where the meeting would be held. The dust clouds headed t(w)oard the frame schoolhouse.

"With Corcoran and his two gundogs attending, this meeting is liable to turn into a free-for-all shooting match," Matt said.

Jean laid her small hand on his as he held the reins. "Honey, we don't need to attend, you know. You have no business there. I asked you to drive out for two reasons."

Wilson listened, eyes on the retreating dust clouds.

"One, I wanted to be alone with you. Two, I wanted to talk over details of my sale with Mr. and Mrs. Volvat. Mr. Volvat is in a wheelchair, as I told you. He gets into town about once every two months. It's hard for him to move. So I'm coming to him, not him to me."

"Has money passed hands?"

"Half has been paid me. I want to rush the deal a little. You don't intend to live in Sageville, do you?"

Wilson closed his eyes. "Please, Jean—no jokes."

The dark-haired, high cheekboned beautiful woman, black of hair and sparkling of eyes, was slowly but surely retreating, Wilson realized. Slipping back into endless time, he reasoned—and strangely, she smiled softly, happily.

He opened his eyes.

Jean's small hand still rested on his knotted fists. Her blue eyes showed worry. "You can do as you wish, Matt. Either turn around, or go ahead."

Matt Juggled the reins. "Get along, ponies. The schoolhouse is ahead."

Jean smiled. She moved closer. Her womanhood pressed against his hard thigh, feminine and curving.

Wilson looked at her. She looked at him.

Wilson said: "One thing is clear to me now."

"Oh? What is that?"

"Why brother Jim fell in love with you!"

Chapter Twelve

The granger meeting was being held to elect a new president. Some claimed nobody would accept the dubious honor, for had not the first two presidents died tragic deaths?

The meeting had just started when Wilson and Jean drove in. Teams hitched to buggies and democrats lined the wooden-rail fence. Saddle-horses waited hip-humped for riders.

Cottonwood trees supported rope swings. Children slid down a wooden slide. Two boys fought, rolling and cursing avidly.

Wilson tied the team, eyes on the fighters. "They sure know the dirty words."

Jean asked: "How old were you when you learned to swear?"

"Four, five, I guess. And you?"

Jean blushed. "I never did learn."

"Try another joke." Wilson looked about. Four saddlehorses—a blue roan, a midnight black, a bay and a sorrel—were tied close together. Wilson recognized the mounts of Sheriff Hanford, Corcoran, Johnson and Griffin.

Wilson breathed deeply. Trouble ahead? Open warfare between Bar Six and the farmers? He wished the quartet had not come. But apparently they were inside, and none was a farmer.

They entered the schoolroom. Farmers stood along

the walls. All benches were filled. Two armed guards were at the door.

"Your pistol, Mr. Wilson. Miss Jean, your rifle. Thank you. John, tag them, put them on hooks."

Jean whispered: "What if they nominate you?"

"If nominated, I'll not run. If elected, I'll not serve."

"Okay, General Sherman, okay."

Johnson and Griffin leaned against the north wall. Wilson looked at the two Bar Six gundogs. Griffin failed to meet his eyes, but Rand Johnson studied Wilson with cold seriousness.

Wilson ironically said: "How are you, Johnson?"

Johnson studied the gambler. Finally he said: "Okay, an' you?"

"Just fine."

The air was tense. A group of women went outside: with Wilson hearing: "There might be gunplay, even with that no-good sheriff on the scene."

"I've begged John to leave. Mr. Smith and Mr. Wilson both died under odd circumstances. We have the children to think of."

"What did your husband say?"

"Under no circumstances will he leave."

The women went outside. A farmer motioned Jean toward the seats the women had vacated. She squeezed Wilson's hand and sat down with other women the farmer had motioned in. Wilson found a seat beside Halversen.

Wilson looked about. He was the only man wearing a suit. All the others wore overalls or levis and common shirts. His shirt was of Canton silk. His boots were the finest Great Falls made.

He was completely out of place.

What was he doing at this meeting of clodhoppers? He disliked Sageville just as he disliked any other gossip-filled little burg. Big cities were corrupt, but small towns were even worse.

Corruption in a big city was usually limited to a few elected officers. In a small town, almost all disliked the others. They hid their dislike under a false cloak of friendship. Then he thought of his brothers and he knew why he was here with this bunch of honyockers. And he knew he'd stay until he discovered the truth. And he was sure what passed for truth was definitely not the truth.

Thick-set Mrs. Warner acted as chairman. When Wilson entered, she had just introduced Sheriff Hanford, who rapped on the table for order.

The room quieted.

The fancy-dressed lawman spoke in a convincing voice. He said law and order would be maintained at all costs. If need be, he would send a special deputy to Sageville.

Jack McKay said: "You'd better send two, Sheriff Hanford, because I am resigned, effective at this minute."

The sheriff asked: "Would you mind telling me why, Mr. McKay?"

"You want the truth?"

"I asked for the truth."

"I refuse any longer to wear a Bart Corcoran collar."

The farmers swung all eyes to Corcoran, who stood in front, to the sheriff's right. There was a moment of tense silence. Then Corcoran wet his lips and clearly said: "Thanks for the dubious compliment, Jack."

McKay spoke to Corcoran. "I'm goin' on record, here an' now, an' I want the record to say that I fear for my life, for Oliver Moe—well, Moe was shot down on the Sageville street right after breakin' with you, Corcoran."

Corcoran said: "A tragic accident, Jack, an' I still hope the killer—whoever he was—is speedily brought to justice."

Sheriff Hanford spoke to Jack McKay. "That's all, Jack?"

McKay sat down. "It was enough, wasn't it?"

The sheriff again rapped. "I'll have a competent deputy sheriff in Sageville by mornin'. I ask all of you—

men, women and children—to let calm heads prevail, the reason I came here. And Mr. Corcoran asked me to come, also so he could present his side of the picture."

"Let 'im talk," a farmer said.

"He could have left his stinkin' gundogs home," a woman said angrily.

The sheriff again pounded with the school's pointer. The meeting was plainly getting out of hand. Mrs. Warner also appealed for order.

Wilson looked at Johnson and Griffin. Griffin had his head down, but Johnson stared stonily straight ahead. Wilson's eyes fell on young Mack Smith, sitting in the next row with his mother and sisters.

The youth lifted his hand slightly. Wilson smiled at him. Wilson liked the youth, although he was a little bit too serious, according to Wilson's summation. But the youth had a right to be serious. He was now the head of the Smith family. Wilson remembered seeing Horace Smith killed.

What would young Mack Smith do if he learned that Rand Johnson had cold-bloodedly murdered his father? Wilson knew. The boy would match guns with Johnson.

And Johnson—an expert gunman—would kill him.

Bart Corcoran took the space behind the desk; the sheriff stepped to one side. The big wealthy cowman stated he had no grudge against the farmers. The three homestead shacks that had mysteriously caught fire when their owners were away was none of Bar Six's doings.

This brought hoots.

Corcoran waited patiently. Matt Wilson wondered if the big cowman was not getting hot under the collar. If and when Corcoran got angry, hot words would fly, Wilson knew.

Corcoran again talked. His Bar Six riders were not responsible for ripped-down barbwire fences and Bar Six cattle trampling down head crops.

"Then who is?" a man demanded.

Corcoran explained that cattle-thieves stole beef in

Northern Montana Territory and drove it south to market across Sageville basin. "They don't go around fences, gentlemen—they merely tear them down."

Wilson realized this allegation held certain merit. He'd read in the *Great Falls Tribune* of such stealing. The sheriff of a county to the south had recently been shot dead from his horse while he and his posse had engaged in a running-gun battle with rustlers.

"Damn off I ain't never seen none of them cowthieves goin' through," a big farmer said, "an' I sit up each night with my rifle to guard my property, Corcoran."

Corcoran did not answer. He spoke to Sheriff Hanford. "I've said my piece. I could tell 'em that a double-eagle was worth twenty bucks and they'd hoot me." He spoke to the farmers. "Thanks for your hospitality."

"You're certainly welcome," a woman said sweetly.

Corcoran started to leave, and Matt Wilson got to his feet and said:"Mr. Corcoran, I believe you'd best hear what I have to say."

Corcoran stopped. Johnson and Griffin, also going toward the door, halted, and Sheriff Hanford, walking behind Corcoran, also stopped and looked at Matt Wilson, who now spoke to Mrs. Warner.

"May I have the floor, Mrs. Warner?"

"Certainly, Mr. Wilson."

Wilson said to the matron: "Pardon me for my abruptness and for speaking without your permission, Madam Chairwoman, but I had to speak fast to keep these men from leaving."

"You are pardoned, Mr. Wilson."

"I definitely want to speak aloud to Mr. Hanford," Matt Wilson said.

"I'm here," the sheriff assured.

Wilson hid his smile. Sheriff Hanford had evidently been counting votes. Maybe he'd decided the farmers owned more votes than did Bart Corcoran and his Bar Six cowpunchers. Anyway, the pudgy lawman seemed extra cordial.

"You will remember my visiting your office in the county seat the other day," Matt Wilson said, "and how I considered my brother to have died under peculiar circumstances, perhaps by murder."

The hall was very quiet.

"I remember, Mr. Wilson."

"I than remarked that the one reason I am on this grass is to settle once and for all the means of my brother's passing. I mentioned I wanted to exhume my brother's body."

A murmur ran through the gathering. Wilson glanced at Bart Corcoran. Corcoran's wide face had no expression. Wilson realized the man would have made a good gambler. His solemn face seldom, if ever, revealed what went on inside the cowman-saloonkeeper.

"I remember," the sheriff said.

"I received permission from you, acting as coroner, to exhume and ship out my brother's body."

"Yes, I gave such permission."

All eyes were on Matt Wilson and Sheriff Hanford.

"I am not totally agreeable to the coroner's findings at the inquest held over my brother's body. I mentioned that to you also. I wish to hold another inquest, with you as coroner in attendance and presiding, this time."

"If I cannot myself attend—if my official duties do not allow me—I shall send a competent doctor of medicine to Sageville to conduct the inquest, Mr. Wilson. Just inform me ahead of time, please."

"That I shall do," Wilson said. "and thanks, sir, for your attention."

"You're welcome, Mr. Wilson." Mr. Wilson." Sheriff Hanford faced the farmers. "I'm at your service, ladies and gentlemen. I bid you good night."

Grangers exchanged glances. The sheriff was very congenial all of a sudden. Evidently he'd counted the heads present. And each head of each adult had been a vote.

Sheriff Hanford and the Bar Six men left. The meeting continued. A farmer slipped in beside Matt Wilson.

"Hanford never rode out with Bar Six. Corcoran an' his two gunnies headed out for Sageville. Hanford rode northwest alone toward the county seat."

"Doesn't mean anything." Wilson reminded. "Corcoran probably had to get to town, Hanford back to his job. Each then had to ride a different direction because of destinations."

"Seems odd, though. Night's here. The county seat's quite a ride off. Take all night to get there."

Wilson nodded. His attention returned to the gathering. Mrs. Warner called for presidential nominations. A number were nominated and all rose to respectfully decline.

Finally Mrs. Warner said: "Somebody nominate me. These men have spines made of jelly."

Jean Benson rose. She nominated Mrs. Warner. Somebody said: "How about Mr. Wilson?" and Matt shook his head. "Under no circumstances. I'm not eligible, either—I've no homestead."

"You own your brother's," a man said.

Wilson shook his head. "I hereby in public give my brother's homestead and all buildings on it to Mrs. Horace Smith. And if tomorrow Mrs. Smith will come to Sageville, I'll sign over the property to her."

Farmers cheered. Mrs. Smith began weeping softly. Young Mack clutched Wilson's hand. "We'll pay you some way, Mr. Wilson."

Wilson laid an arm around thin shoulders. "You'll have to catch me, Mack—and it's a long way to Macao."

"I know where Macao is, Mr. Wilson. It's a Portugese colony off the China coast, across from Hong Kong. I liked geography."

"Or on the Riviera," Wilson said.

The boy smiled. "In other words, Mr. Wilson—no pay?"

"Be kind to your mother and sisters, and I'll have pay enough."

Wilson wanted to leave. He disliked emotional

scenes. Some lingered over saying farewell. He never did. He just said goodbye and left.

Mrs. Warner said, "Miss Benson nominated me for the Grange presidency. All nominations need a second. Who will second her nomination?"

"I will," a woman said.

"The nomination has been made and seconded," Mrs. Warner said. "Now the voting shall begin. All in favor of my being Grange president say *aye*, please."

"*Aye!*"

"All not in favor say *no*."

Silence.

"Then I am elected," the woman said.

Wilson held Jean's elbow as they pushed toward the door. "Did you finish your business with the Volvats?" Wilson asked.

"They come to town tomorrow to pay all."

Outside, the stars were blue, distant. Later, there'd be a moon. Farmers now were also leaving, the meeting adjourned.

Wilson untied the sorrels. Jean said: "I didn't like it. A woman having to declare herself a candidate. And big healthy men sitting there apparently too scared."

Wilson helped her into the rig. He then handed her the reins while he climbed onto the spring seat beside her. She handed him the reins and he backed up the team, breeching straps tight against the horses' flanks.

He straightened the Rochester. "Why say that?"

"Women should stay at home and rear children and keep house. Men should be the providers and the fighters."

Wilson remembered seeing a few sleek, well-tailored women fighting at his tables. "I don't agree," he said, "but let's not discuss it. At least I doubt if Corcoran will kill a woman."

"He does that and this grass will explode. Some still wonder whether or not you actually saw Rand Johnson kill Horace Smith."

"I suppose so."

108

Jean didn't ask confirmation. Evidently she knew he'd not give her a *yes* or *no*. And she'd guessed right. Wilson had a hole-card. And you don't tip your hole-card up until the final showdown.

The team started at a fast trot toward Sageville. Suddenly the rig was surrounded by riders. One farmer leaned low and hollered: "We'll escort you into town, Wilson."

"Why?"

The farmer waved his arm to take in the huge expanse. "Lots of brush out there. And maybe Corcoran—or some of his gunnies—might not want you to dig up Jim."

"They've got a point," said Jean.

One farmer gave out a Blackfoot war whoop. Others answered in kind. The buggy team began to run. The trot broke into a gallop. They rocked down the lane, dust rising, farmers whooping.

Wilson let the team run. The road was bumpy. The buggy swayed. Jean clung to his arm. She smiled up at him.

"You're a popular man, Mr. Wilson."

"I'm glad somebody likes me."

She pressed his arm. "I've liked you since the first time I saw you, Mr. Wilson."

"That goes two ways," Matt Wilson said.

Chapter Thirteen

Bart Corcoran and his two gunmen left the schoolhouse headed northwest toward Bar Six, but two miles out in the sagebrush the cowman pulled his black to a rough halt, right hand raised to stop his riders.

Rand Johnson reined in his bronc. "What's on your mind Bart?"

"That sheriff— hell, he was almost huggin' them hoemen when he left. You could see the bastard countin' heads. He's so stupid his lips move when he reads or counts."

"He had to act that way," said Johnson. "That meetin' was ready to explode. We shouldn't have gone there. We was damn lucky to get out alive. An' what did we accomplish?"

"I went on record as sayin' I wasn't against the grangers, for one thing. I showed the sheriff just what Bar Six was buckin'."

Johnson laughed sardonically. "An' what did Hanford do?" He answered his own question. "Started kissin' babies for votes."

Mel Griffin sat his horse in silence. Griffin was deadly afraid of Bart Corcoran. He'd seen Corcoran in action. The man was ruthless, a murderer at heart—money-mad and unscrupulous.

Despite the heat, Mel Griffin shivered slightly. Should of brought my jumper with me, he told himself.

Corcoran was the type who'd silently lay a Winchester .30-30 across a windowsill, take careful aim in the moonlight, then send a bullet through the back of a sleeping man's brain, Griffin realized.

Corcoran said, "Who's runnin' this show, Johnson?" You or me?"

"You are, Bart."

"All right, I'll ask you what'd you do?"

Johnson put his big hands on his saddle's fork. He rocked on stirrups for a long moment. He remembered two men in the alley. One man had turned to untie his team.

The other had put his short-gun against this man's back. He'd pulled the trigger. He'd sent a steel-jacketed bullet through the man's heart from behind.

And at that moment a stranger—a damned gambler—had come around a corner. Had the gambler seen him murder Horace Smith?

If he had, what he'd seen could send a man—Randolf Johnson—to the gallows.

"I'd kill this Wilson bucko," Johnson said, "an' I'd kill him tonight, if possible—or as soon as possible."

Bart Corcoran debated. He sat a solid saddle—a big, dangerous man on a tough stud. Wind sang in the sagebrush. The smell of a bog down around Doggone Creek was strong. It assailed your nostrils.

The wind shifted. The bog stink left. Johnson pressed his point. "Wilson holds the key. With him dead, his brother won't be dug up. You'll be out of danger from that point, boss."

Corcoran said: "Watch your tongue, Rand."

Johnson laughed. "There's only us three here. Bart, you're jumpy, man. Only us three know."

Bart Corcoran looked slantingly at Mel Griffin. Griffin caught the significance of the glance. Three who knew might be one too many. The cold spot grew in Mel Griffin's guts. Griffin wanted to ride out. He remembered Oliver Moe, though—the shot from a deserted building, Moe clutching his belly, going down dead.

112

Corcoran had gunmen watching all the people going in and out of Sageville.

Johnson continued. "Matt Wilson is the only danger Bar Six has, Bart. The farmers are all yellow. They's no danger in them. None of 'em will run for president."

"How'd you know?" Corcoran asked. "We left before they began votin'."

"I listened to the scissorbills. Every man I heard talk said under no circumstances would he be elected president. They remember Jim Wilson an' Horace Smith."

"Maybe Wilson saw you kill Smith," said Corcoran.

Johnson shrugged. "What if he did? He saw a fair-and square gunfight. I even let Smith drag gun first. Then I drew, an' I kilt him. I only wish Wilson had seen it. He'd have to testify I shot in defense of my life."

"I agree with Rand," Mel Griffin said.

Corcoran turned on Griffin. "Who asked you to stick in your oar, Griffin? Nobody asked your opinion. Look, weren't the gambler and Jean Benson the only people who drove out from Sageville?"

Johnson looked at his boss. "They were the only ones from Sageville. All the others were farmers from their farms. Why ask, Bart?"

Bart Corcoran did not answer right away. He seemed to be in a deep and brown study.

Griffin looked at Johnson. Johnson stared into the starlight. A horse shifted, hoofs grating dust.

Finally Bart Corcoran said: "What if their team ran away, an' they both got kilt in the runaway? Nobody would come along until tomorrow to find them, seein' nobody else from Sageville was there."

"Best to have bodies without bullet holes," Johnson said.

Corcoran said: "No bullet holes. Clubbed to death while lyin' on the ground, but no bullet holes."

Griffin leaned forward, saddle leather creaking. "Look, men—I got a plan. We get their team runnin' wild. Then we shoot one of their broncs. He goes down, an' the buggy goes over him, an' they get throwed out

113

an—"

"An' we hope they get killed," Johnson finished.

Griffin settled back. "Damn it, is my opinion worth nothin' to you two bastards?"

Corcoran laughed. Johnson said: "My mother an' father was married, Mel, so I'm no bastard. They even had their wedding license framed on the wall."

"I take it back," said Griffin.

Johnson said: "Better. Much better."

"On the Sageville school road?" Corcoran asked. "Where's the highest brush?"

Rand Johnson leaned back in saddle. "Tanner's Ridge, of course. Sagebrush so high there it can hide the tallest steer. A man has to use a catch-dog to run the wild-uns out. He can't see 'em."

"Tanner's Ridge," Corcoran said.

They turned broncs southwest. They followed a trail made by Bar Six cattle going down to water in Doggone Creek's sinking water supply. Corcoran heard the pathetic bawling of a cow off to the northeast.

Sounded like a cow caught in a bog along Doggone. The bawl had that desolate sound about it. He'd get a cowhand to check the bog come morning. He went over the salient points.

Johnson was right. With Wilson out of the way, much of the trouble on this grass would have evaporated. Of course, the woman would have to be killed, too. They'd leave no witness behind. They couldn't affort to leave any.

Corcoran led the way, riding high in leather, his big stud's steel-shod hoofs pounding Montana's parched earth. A pace behind, on the Bar Six owner's right, rode his top gun, Rand Johnson.

Bart Corcoran glanced left, where pounded Mel Griffin, the weak link. There and then he made a promise he would kill Griffin as soon as time and circumstance allowed.

Corcoran figured the Sageville-schoolhouse road was three miles south. Bar Six now approached Tanner's

Ridge. Here the wagon trail crossed a summit, the one on which Wilson's buggy had rested when Bar Six and the sheriff had swept past, heading for Sageville Basin school.

Here, too, Rand Johnson had fired over Wilson's head, an insulting gesture. Suddenly, Bart Corcoran pulled in his hard-running stud, boots jamming deep in Visalia stirrups, right hand shooting out to stop his two gunmen. "What the hell's that ungodly racket?"

Johnson cocked his ugly head to listen better. "Sounds like a bunch of riders, boss."

"I know that," Corcoran growled, "but what are riders doin' out in this wilderness this time of night?

"Sounds like they's headed for Sageville," Griffin said.

"What the hell do you use for brains?" Corcoran asked.

"Naturally they're headin' for town. They're comin' closer, not goin' away. Wonder where a man can get a clear look at the trail? This high sagebrush hides everythin."

Griffin jabbed a thumb northwest. "There's a high ridge there, boss. Lots of big boulders a man can hide behind. When I hunt dogies out here I get on the ridge and use my fieldglasses to spot the critters. From the brush, a man couldn't see a single one."

"Lead the way," Corcoran ordered.

A few minutes later, hidden by big granite boulders, the wagon road lay clearly below and to the south a hundred yards. Riders roared along it, headed for Sageville, and in their midst was a buggy, its team running hard, dust spinning upward behind to lie gray and dead against the Montana starlight.

"That Wilson's rig?" Corcoran asked.

Johnson nodded. "Sure looks like it, boss. He drove the girl's Rochester. Jean's team, too."

"What d'you suppose is goin' on?" Mel Griffin asked.

Corcoran growled: "Simple, you dunce. Wilson was afraid we might ambush him. So he gets the farmers to ride with him into Sageville."

"They're sure hollerin'," Griffin said. "They put the coyotes to shame. Ride 'em cowboy stuff, huh?"

Corcoran could only nod. Anger welled up inside the big man. He'd hoped to finish Wilson off, once and for always.

"We ride down there," Griffin said, "an' they'll shoot us into mincemeat, boss."

"You don't say," Corcoran scoffed. "You don't say."

Mel Griffin glanced at his boss. He realized that once again he'd made a slip of tongue. He had always been somewhat afraid of Bart Corcoran. Now that fear was steadily growing into naked terror.

He decided to keep his mouth shut. He'd watch carefully, and the time and right place would arrive, he felt sure.

Bar Six watched the farmers and buggy until all fell from sight in the starlight against the distance. Finally there was only the endless sea of gray sage and the eternal wind.

Corcoran said: "Griffin, you head for Bar Six. Tell Smoky to ride Doggone Crick's bogs come mornin'. I think I heard a critter bogged down when we turned to ride this direction."

"I heard him, too," Griffin said.

Corcoran said: "Get movin', Mel."

Griffin turned his bronc and said: "Hold down the fort, gentlemen," and loped northwest. Rand Johnson's mount pulled at the bit, rolling the cricket. Bart Corcoran sat deep in leather, seemingly in profound thought.

Johnson waited patiently.

Finally Bart Corcoran said: "We ride into town. I can't keep my finger on things from the ranch."

He turned his horse. He rode downhill, gross body pulled by gravity, with Johnson riding behind, body balanced against thrust-out stirrups. They reached the hill's bottom.

With Corcoran heading, they rode at a lope straight west. Johnson fitted his tough body to his horse's rocking gait. Sageville lay southwest, and they rode directly west.

Johnson knew why.

Soon the riders would sweep out of Sageville, heading for each one's homestead. And by riding due west, he and Corcoran would hit the Bar Six—Sageville trail at the base of Thunder Butte.

Thunder Butte reared its dark, igneous crest west of the trail. At its base, they'd turn their mounts south, thus entering Sageville from the north. Thus, they'd meet no farmers.

For the farmers would all ride northeast.

Once on the Sageville road, the pair pulled mounts to a fast running walk. Here the rimrock broke the wind. Two jackrabbits jumped from concealment under greasewood, and Bart Corcoran's horse shied, almost throwing Corcoran.

Corcoran hammered the bronc over the head with the shot-loaded butt of his quirt, giving the horse a brutal beating. Johnson said nothing. He'd seen a man kill a horse by hitting him so.

The stud reared, forehooves pawing. He wanted to buck off this human monster. Corcoran knew horses. You control a horse's head and you control the horse.

So he reined the stud into a spin, all the time beating the animal over the head. Finally, the defeated animal straightened out, all its fight gone.

The moon's yellow rays showed Corcoran's mean, twisted face. He spurred the stud into a savage gallop. The animal ran with whipping tail, dancing mane.

Johnson rode a fast horse, too—Johnson rode abreast, solid in stirrups. Horses thundered on in the moonlight.

Then Sageville lay ahead.

Dark, squalid, Sageville hugged the Montana prairie, its only light the yellow lamps of Corcoran's Montana House.

Only then did Bar Six pull in foam-flecked mounts.

Chapter Fourteen

Next morning Melvin Griffin ate his ham and eggs alone in Bar Six's big dining room. Because he and Johnson were gunmen and because Bart Corcoran always wanted a bodyguard close to him, he and Johnson slept in the ranch house, a privilege and honor awarded not even Bar Six's foreman.

Bart had shipped in a new squaw. This one was only about fourteen, Griffin figured, if that old. Evidently Bart broke them in younger these days. Griffin smiled over his fork.

"Where'd Runnin' Deer go?" he asked.

"Me no talkem white mans talk."

The squaw returned to her kitchen. Griffin admired her thin waist and feminine hips. He shoved such thoughts reluctantly aside, and concentrated on his breakfast.

The little girl was a good cook, he saw. Eggs just right, sunny-side up, ham done to a turn. Somewhere she'd learned to cook. Mel Griffin gobbled down the victuals.

He's spent a sleepless night. At dawn, a cowboy had ridden in from Sageville. The cowpoke had been drunk. He'd been singing *Sweet Adeline* loud enough to wake up the dead.

"Hey, Mel pal," he hollered.

Grudgingly, Mel had called him to his bedroom window. The cowboy's bronc was lathered. "Bart an' Rand got two new girls, Mel," the cowboy had reported.

"What's that to me?"

"Good lookers, both. One blonde, t'other dark. They druv a buggy overland from Miles City."

"Long way across the sagebrush. Now go to bed, Joe. Tell Smoky come mornin' to ride over to Doggone Bogs. Bart done tol' me he figgered some stock might be stuck down there. Bart heard 'em bawlin', he said."

"I'll tell 'im. Some stiffs have all the luck."

"What d'you mean by that?"

"Bart an' Rand. Then two new heifers—"

The cowboy went to turn his horse. He fell from saddle into the flower bed beneath the bedroom window. His fall trampled the morning glories and petunias there.

"Bart'd kill you if he knowed you fell into his flowers," Mel Griffin said, "cause if there's one thing Bart likes, it's his flower beds."

"Here, I'll stand this one up straight."

"Get to your bunk, Joe."

Joe staggered off, leading his horse, and still singing *Sweet Adeline.* Mel Griffin had returned to bed, but sleep would not come.

He wished he didn't know as much as he knew. Or that he'd seen as much as he'd seen. But he knew what he knew—and he'd seen what he'd seen—and that was that.

And a man couldn't forget very fast. And what he'd seen he'd seen and he couldn't go back and miss seeing what he'd seen.

Finally, broken sleep came. And now, red-eyed from yesterday's booze, bleary-eyed from lack of sleep, young Melvin Griffin toyed with his ham and eggs and faced his dour thoughts.

Breakfast finished, he carried his dirty dishes into the kitchen, where the young Assiniboine ate standing up at the stove. He put his dishes in the sink and, in passing, playfully slapped her on the behind.

She turned quickly, face angry, and slapped at his face. He leaped back, surprised. She was very, very angry. For a moment her dark and savage eyes glared into his startled blue eyes.

One moment was enough. In her eyes he read the hate one race has for another, and he suddenly felt sorry for Custer when he'd run into the combined Sioux-Cheyenne down on the Little Big Horn some ten years or more back.

Custer must have seen hundreds of such hate-filled eyes before the battle-axe split his skull.

"You take life seriously, sister."

"Go, white bastard!"

Mel Griffin smiled crookedly. "You tol' me you never understood English, remember? Bart will take care of 'you. He'll tame you or kill you."

Maybe he spoke the truth. A number of squaws had mysteriously disappeared on Bar Six.

He bathed, shaved, polished his boots. About nine he rode out on a high-stepping dappled gray gelding, heading for Sageville.

He took his time, gray running-walking, his master thinking of two men—Matt Wilson and Bartholemew Corcoran.

Wilson had really laid the pistol barrel to him the day Wilson had taken over his brother's farm. He'd called him to draw and he'd started his draw, but Wilson had been far, far ahead.

Wilson had been so far ahead he'd had no need to fire. He'd merely stepped in, six-shooter raised, and pistol-whipped him.

Wilson was a heller with a six-gun.

His thoughts ran to Corcoran. Corcoran could draw, level, fire—and fast, too. Corcoran practiced each day. Either back of his Montana House or out on his ranch. Corcoran, Johnson and Griffin practiced together.

Johnson was fast, but Johnson lacked Corcoran's accuracy. Corcoran was chained-lightning combined with accuracy. And, according to Mel Griffin, accuracy was

121

perhaps more important than rapidity.

Mel Griffin was no fast gun, and he knew it. He ranked behind Johnson, who in turn was behind Bart Corcoran. He knew that Corcoran would not fire him. Corcoran could not allow him to ride out unscathed. He knew too much. Corcoran would kill him first.

Mel Griffin's belly was ice.

He rode past Sageville's cemetery. Matt Wilson was walking among the graves. Wilson stopped him. "Which is my brother's grave?"

Griffin frowned. He felt sure Wilson had known the location of Jim Wilson's grave, but had merely wanted to stop him.

"That one there."

Griffin pointed to a fresh mound on Wilson's right. "Where are Applegate and Moe buried?" Wilson asked.

Griffin pointed north. "There, in that section. It's sorta apart, as you kin see. That's called Boothill."

"That's where they bury Corcoran's bum gunmen, huh?"

Griffin nodded. Which did he fear the most: Corcoran or Wilson? He decided on Corcoran. Corcoran had no scruples, no code of honesty, of ethics. Corcoran killed when he wanted. If ambush suited him, then it was ambush. And ambush was Corcoran's preference.

Wilson fought openly, fairly, squarely.

"You goin' dig up your brother?" Griffin asked.

Wilson's blue eyes studied Griffin. Griffin felt uneasy under their steady gaze. He did not know that Wilson was deliberately judging his inner stamina.

For Wilson earned his living evaluating the abilities and mettle of other humans. And he had already catalogued Mel Griffin as the weakest link in Bart Corcoran's chain of gunnies.

"I kinda like you," Wilson said.

Griffin was surprised. "You damn' near beat me to death with your pistol," he said," an' now you like me. I don't understand."

122

"A person can let bygones by bygones," said Wilson.

Griffin nodded. "I kin understan' that. Be kinda messy diggin' up a man thet's been dead as long as your brother, won't it?"

"It'll be worth it, I think."

Griffin asked: "In what way, Mr. Wilson?"

Wilson played his ace. "I look at it this way, Griffin. I'm sure my brother was murdered, shot from the window when he slept—and shot in the back of the head."

Griffin nodded, listening.

"The night was hot. The calendar shows full moon at that time. He went to sleep and forgot to pull the shade on the window. He slept with his back to the window."

"What makes you think he was shot?"

"I saw powder marks on the window sill. I'd say the assassin tipped his rifle slightly. When he shot, powder burned the wooden sill a little."

Griffin's blood raced. This man was a genius. He could really put two and two together, and he always got four. "You got any idea who kilt him?" he asked slowly.

"I got suspicions," Wilson said.

Griffin shifted in leather. "I was to the coroner's inquest. I saw your brother's head. It had only one bullet hole in it. An' they was powder marks aroun' the wound, like he'd been shot from the front at mighty close range, Mr. Wilson."

"That's easy to explain. The bullet came out Jim's forehead. The killer then shot into the same hole with Jim's .45."

"You mean they'd be two holes in the back of his head?"

"That's right. One where the killer's bullet went in, one where the bullet from Jim's gun came out."

Griffin rubbed his bottom lip. "You might have a point there, Mr. Wilson. Yep, you just might have one, sir."

"You ever seen the back of Jim's head when the coroner held his inquest?"

Griffin shook his head. "Nope. He had your brother covered by a big piece of cloth. He pulled it down just enough so we could see his face."

"The deputy who acted as coroner— he a good friend of Bart Corcoran's, maybe?"

Griffin's heart missed a beat. "They're on rather good terms, yes—but I don't know the deputy well enough to say how strong the terms are. I'd best get to town. So long, Mr. Wilson."

"So long, Griffin."

Mel Griffin put the dappled gray to a long lope. This thing was getting hot, he reasoned. Matt Wilson had recited, almost action for action, how his brother had been murdered.

He glanced back. Matt Wilson stood looking down at his brother's grave. Griffin rode into the town livery barn, and Wilson walked slowly back to Jean Benson's cafe.

He took a seat in the first booth. From there, he could watch both back and front doors. The cafe had but one customer—a cowboy eating hotcakes and eggs at the counter.

Wilson judged the cowpoke to be a rider drifting through. This drought was widespread, even into Canada. Many outfits were cutting back on their payrolls. Thus, cowboys had become drifters.

Jean was instructing Mrs. Volvat on the cafe's operation. Mr. Volvat was back polishing the big Kalamazoo stove.

Jean came over with a cup of coffee and two doughnuts. She slid into the booth opposite him. Their eyes met. She smiled softly. Wilson found himself smiling back.

She was what he had searched for. Marie was moving back into time and space and losing significance, as she had said she would. Wilson was glad he had ridden into Sageville, if only because of Jean.

"Where have you been?" she asked.

"Cemetery. Jim's grave."

She frowned. "Jim is dead, darling. Were he alive, he'd ask you not to worry."

Matt Wilson said: "I can't ride away without knowing. I can't turn my back on my obligations to my only brother."

"I don't mean it that way, Matt. But you're alive. Jim isn't. We all have to lose our loved ones. I have lost both my mother and father. But I have to go on. And so do you."

Odd—but Marie had said the same.

Jean got to her feet. "Wilson's Man," she said.

"He's on my right shoulder. He never leaves me."

She kissed his forehead. "Wilson's Man is part my man now." Her face sobered. "Well, got to get to work."

Wilson walked outside. He stood for a moment on the plank sidewalk, looking at Sageville's dusty street and unpainted buildings. The only building in town with new paint was Corcoran's Montana House.

Wilson smiled. He had learned one point early in life: crime pays, if the right authorities are bought off. And evidently Bartholomew Corcoran—and his father before him—knew and had known the right palms to rub with silver.

Rand Johnson left the Montana House and took a seat on one of the long porch benches, legs stretched out.

Ironically, Wilson lifted a hand. Johnson did not wave back. Wilson turned and walked toward his living quarters behind the hardware store.

He spat out his toothpick.

He had a hunch that things were drawing to a point, and at that point would be gunsmoke. His talk with Mel Griffin, he figured, might be the pivot upon which further events rotated.

One thing stood out, for sure. Bart Corcoran could not permit him tp remain in Sageville. The longer he remained, the lesser grew Corcoran's hold over Sageville.

For he had called Corcoran's hand. And if Corcoran didn't respond, Corcoran would have lost.

And the response, Wilson figured, would be with gunsmoke.

Rain came that afternoon

Chapter Fifteen

The rain came from the northwest. It did not come as a cloudburst. It came gently, with the first drops big and wet. It settled into a steady, penetrating rainfall—just what the land and the farmers' crops needed.

Had it come as a cloudburst it would have done much damage, for the earth was bone-dry and would have washed away easily into gullies and creeks. A cloudburst would have swept young plants and seeds away.

Farmers went wild.

They stood in the rain with open, bearded mouths, hollering in pure delight. Were this rain to continue but two days, their head crops would be saved. Alfalfa would grow rapidly.

Of course, the rain was late. Unless they had a very late fall, wheat would not have time to ripen. Oats would, but not wheat and barley. Wheat and barley needed a longer growing season.

But if the rain continued for a couple of days they'd be assured of plenty of winter hay for their livestock. Those crops that didn't mature would be cut and stacked and fed to cows and horses during the winter blizzards. Either way, the farmers were bound to win.

Also, rain would raise the prairie grass high. It could be mowed and stacked for winter feed, too.

They'd made an agreement that if rain ever came they'd all meet at the schoolhouse. They came on foot, on horseback, in open buggies and wagons, all soaked to the skin, all happy, all joking, pounding each other—and wanting something stronger than rainwater.

A light springwagon pulled by two fast sorrels headed out for the county seat. It made record time. When it returned, it carried five barrels of beer. During the interim, farmers had been drinking home brew made by Hans Hanover, a transplanted Prussian.

Hans had a plentiful supply of beer. By the time the buggy returned, almost all of the farmers were pleasantly drunk.

Some wives and mother pleaded with their menfolks not to get drunk, but their pleas fell on deaf ears.

Some of the women got drunk with their men. Mrs. Horace Smith was very proud of her boy, Mack, for Mack drank very little. "Somebody has to take care of these fools," he told his mother. "I hope they don't break out fightin'."

"Oh, that terrible alcohol," the widow said. "Your dead father, son—a splendid man, but about once a year— well, he'd fall off the water wagon, as he himself said."

"Johnson didn't kill Dad in a fair fight."

"How can you say that? Were you there to see it?"

"No, but Wilson was."

"Mr. Wilson says he came after your father was dead." Fear touched the woman's voice. "Son, what are you thinking?"

Nothing, Mama."

"There are times when your face— let your father rest in peace, son. He'd want it that way."

"I can't agree, mama."

"You're like your father. Stubborn, set in your ways. I tried to talk him out of becomin' the president of the Grange. But, oh, no—and you see what happened."

"Somebody had to be president. Somebody has to stand up in front of Corcoran."

"Why?"

"Because if somebody doesn't kill him, he'll kill some

of us. You don't seem to understand, Mama."

"Oh, I understand. But I'm afraid, son, afraid."

"Everybody is afraid but Matt Wilson."

"A great, brave man, Mr. Wilson. But I fear for him—Corcoran, and that terrible gunman, Johnson— and the other thing, Griffin—"

One farmer said the celebration should be transferred to Sageville. "Mr. Wilson might want to be in on the fun."

"He doesn't drink. Never touches a drop."

"Must be a reformed drunkard," Hans Hanover said. "When they quit, they're against all others boozin'."

"I'm the same way about tobacco. Used to smoke a pipe, cigarettes, cigars— what have you. Then I quit. Now I try to talk everybody else who smokes into quittin'."

"You chew plenty, though, I notice."

"I kain't get away from the weed. Hell, yes, let's get into town. Celebrate in the hardware store."

So the group moved into Sageville late that night. They hammered on Matt Wilson's door. Wilson responded, wearing only his b.v.d.'s. Under no circumstances would he take a drink.

"Sure, you can throw your drunk in the hardware store. It's mine no longer. It belongs to you farmers."

"If we can pay for it, yes," one said.

Another said: "Stop such talk, Nels. You know the finances of the deal and they favor us all the way."

"Cy's right. No more such talk, Nels."

"All right, all right. Don't chew my ears off."

The farmers drunkenly lurched toward the hardware store's back door, Mack Smith staying a while to tell Matt Wilson: "I'm kinda overseein' the thing, I guess. Mama an' me."

"Your mother?" Wilson asked.

"She and Miss Jean are makin' coffee and grub in Miss Jean's cafe. They're goin' to feed the men, to try to sober them up."

Wilson nodded. "Nice rain, Mack."

"Wonderful rain. We all spent last night in Jim's house, Mr. Wilson. That sure is a nice house."

"I'm glad you like it, Mack."

Young Mack Smith advanced with the drunks into the front part of the hardware store, where men took seats on benches and the floor and against the walls while three men carried in the three remaining barrels of beer.

Men went to the barrels carrying their glasses. Wilson returned to his sleeping quarters.

He closed the door. He leaned against it. He heard the voices of the farmers. Rain hammered loudly on the tin roof.

He leaned against the door, thinking.

He had a hunch this trouble was coming to a head, and all his life he'd lived—and been directed—by hunches.

What would the finish be? There was but one answer.

Gunsmoke . . . .

Corcoran would permit no other ending.

Wilson sucked damp air deep into his lungs. Maybe it had not been good luck—but bad—when he'd met Jean Benson.

Facts were simple. Guns killed people. A gun could kill him. Jean could become bereaved before even being married.

What foolishness was he thinking? Of course he could be killed. Then, again, he wasn't sure of being killed. He remembered nights—tragic, lonely nights—after Marie's death.

With Jean, those nights would be gone forever.

Somebody pounded on the door. Jack McKay stood there in the rain. "You know what's goin' on, don't you?"

Matt Wilson nodded.

"I quit my job jus' in time. Good Lord, Wilson, this town has no law."

Wilson was on the point of telling the ex-deputy it had had no law while he'd toted a star, but held back the words.

130

"Somebody start talkin' fight to these hoemen and they might march on the Montana House and try to take Corcoran an' his gang apart. This is serious, Wilson."

Matt Wilson admitted it was. "But what can we do?"

"Get word into the county seat. Get the sheriff to work."

Matt Wilson laughed sardonically. "You are an optimist, McKay. Hanford washed his hands of Sageville last night at the schoolhouse meeting."

McKay spread his hands. "I guess you're right. Hell, I *know* you're right, Wilson."

"We just got to wait," Wilson said.

"I'm goin' talk to Corcoran," McKay said, and left.

McKay found Corcoran in his upstairs room. Corcoran said: "Hell, I know they're in town. I know most are drunk. I know there's no legal law, except what a man packs in his fists and his holster."

"Maybe if you got outa town—"

Corcoran laughed. "You talk like a damned idiot, McKay! You talked an' acted just as stupid when I had you wearin' a star. I get out of town an' Montana House will be ablaze the minute I top that big ridge two miles north on the road to Bar Six."

McKay shrugged. "I tried," he said.

Corcoran had narrowed, dangerous eyes. He said: "I'm goin' to do somethin' I've wanted to do for a long, long time."

McKay's brows rose. "An' thet, Corcoran?"

"Kick your butt all the way out into the street!"

McKay ducked. Too late. Corcoran's right hit his jaw solidly. McKay sagged, stunned but not out. Corcoran grabbed the ex-deputy by the shoulders.

Corcoran's eyes had an insane look. He chortled with glee as his right boot landed solidly against McKay's buttocks. McKay lurched from the room, staggering into the hall.

Corcoran's foot rose again. This kick propelled McKay to the stairway. McKay grabbed for the stairpost. He caught it steadied himself, and said, "Bart, for the love of—"

Blood showed on McKay's lips.

Bart Corcoran kicked him again. McKay went flying down the stairs, to land in a heap in the saloon.

Rand Johnson and Mel Griffin sat a table, glasses and bottle beside their elbows. McKay's scream turned them, and both instinctively dropped hands to holstered guns.

"Hell," Johnson growled. "Bart jus' havin' a bit of fun, Mel."

Griffin said nothing. His eyes were pulled down in thought. He watched Corcoran kick the hollering McKay across the saloon and out the door into the muddy street.

"What's eatin' you, Mel?" Johnson asked.

Griffin came to earth. "What'd you mean?"

"You're thinkin', man—an' thinkin' don't fit your face one bit," Johnson joked.

Without thinking, Griffin said: "Hell's goin' bust loose any minute now, an' I'd like to get out."

"Don't let Bart hear you say that."

"What would he do?"

"He'd kill you," Rand Johnson said.

Chapter Sixteen

Corcoran brushed off his hands. He went to the bar. Johnson and Griffin moved in on each side.

Griffin said: "Never saw you so mad, Bart."

"I can get madder."

"When the boys comin' in from the ranch?" Johnson asked.

Corcoran threw down a slug of old Horseshoe. "Some of the bastards backed out. When Thaddeus told them about this trouble about half of them saddled up and rode out—headin' north!"

"They leave for good?" Griffin asked.

"Naturally, you fool."

Griffin had no reply. Johnson said: "They should be due any minute here in town, I reckon. Them that didn't light out, I mean."

"You got cold boots?" Corcoran asked.

"No, but— those hoemen are boozed up. They out number us way t'hell an' gone."

"Let 'em come," Corcoran said, "We're armed strong. Dozen or so shotguns behind the bar. All loaded with birdshot an' buckshot. One blast of one of them, an' at least two farmers go down."

"The two bartenders?" Johnson asked. "They sidin' us?"

Corcoran said: "You white-aprons. In a tight, you handle weapons along with us boys?"

"All the way, Bart."

"Count me in, boss."

Griffin said: "Reckon I'll head up to my quarters, boss. Stitchin' broke a bit on my holster an' I'd best mend it. Damn wish this rain would quit. If this danged rain hadn't come, mebbe the dry spell would have driven out these damned farmers!"

"Go up an' shine your boots!" Bart Corcoran snarled. the stairs. Johnson said quietly: "Everythin's gone wrong since that gambler rode into town. Who the hell do you figure killed Walt Byron?"

"That Smith kid."

"You mean young Mack Smith? Horace's son?"

"That's who I mean. Jake Slocum was ridin' that country the day Byron got killed. Jake was lookin' for strays. He seen the kid in that area. An' he never saw nobody else right aroun' where Byron had hid himself."

"What about McKay an' the gambler that day?"

"Jake told me they rode wide of that spot that day, I guess 'cause they saw Byron hidin'. Jake was on Smuggler's Butte watchin' with field glasses for Bar Six cows. He saw it all by accident. He's sure young Smith sneaked up on Byron and killed him."

Johnson considered this. "Possible, an' probable. Young Smith thinks the world of the gambler. He'd do anythin' for him."

Corcoran refilled his glass. "Maybe he's Wilson's Man?" He grinned crookedly. "You've heard about Wilson's Man, ain't you?"

"Yeah . . . . Wilson's luck piece, I guess you'd call him. Lotta crap to me. Griffin, now . . . ."

Corcoran put down his empty glass. "What about Griffin?"

"I was down the livery checkin' my horse when Griffin rode in from the ranch this mornin'. From the stable's back door a man can see the graveyard, you know."

"Go on."

"Griffin stops an' talks with the gambler. Wilson's

lookin' over his brother's grave, I guess. Maybe before he starts diggin' up the carcass."

"Continue."

"They jawed quite a spell, boss. Real friendly-like, I'd say."

Corcoran made damp circles with his glass. From outside came the sudden howl of a Blackfoot buck on warpath. The farmers were really whooping it up, Corcoran thought sourly.

"That don't make sense," Corcoran finally said. "Wilson pistol-whipped the crap out of Griffin when he took over his brother's homestead."

"That don't mean nothin'."

"I get what you mean, Johnson. Griffin might think the farmers'll win, an' he wants to be on the winnin' side."

Johnson nodded. "He might turn tail an' report back to Wilson what you're doin' an' figgerin' to do—you know."

"He remembers Oliver Moe," Corcoran said. "He knows how long Moe lived after he hollered about desertin'."

Johnson said: "A beer, Olaf," and then: Well, he's your man, boss. You pay his wages, not me."

Corcoran turned his big head. He stared moodily out the front windows. "Danged rain is comin' down harder. Wish it'd turn into a cloudburst an' wash thet whole caboodle into Doggone Crick."

But the rain didn't turn into a downpour. It fell steadily, with every little wind. Therefore there was little runoff. The glad earth somberly but thoroughly soaked up moisture.

And, in the hardware store, the jubilant farmers soaked up Great Falls beer.

Jean and the wives and daughters cooked for them in Jean's cafe. At first they figured that food might sober up their husbands and sons, but they were fooled in this attempt.

The farmers ate everything the women served them

and then licked plates and asked for more, but as they ate they drank, foamy mugs and glasses of beer at their elbows.

They got no more sober. In fact, Jean figured they got drunker.

The women then tried to steal the remaining kegs of beer. This they could not do. Farmers came to the rescue of their brew. The women were forced out of the store.

Mrs. Volvat broke out laughing. "If this wasn't so serious it would be comical."

"Comedy is akin to tragedy," Mrs. Smith said. "Where's my son, Mack?"

"He's with the men in the store. No, he's not drinking," a matron said. "He's just a sort of guardian over the drunks, like Mr Wilson is. You're gettin' a wonderful man, Jean. I wish my Wilbur never drank a drop, but he does. Oh, not much, but twice a year he goes on a toot."

"I think he's great," Jean said.

"Your boy has aged since his father got killed," a woman told the Widow Smith. "He was a boy a few days ago—now he's a man. He's so sober, and he has such a somber face now."

Mrs. Smith said: "I don't like his actions a bit. Not a whit, Missus Breckinridge. He's gone a lot from home. I thought when we moved into the nice new house—the one Mr. Wilson gave us—the one Mr. Wilson's brother built—" The widow was close to tears.

The others waited.

Finally the widow said: "Last night he just stood there—outside the house—and he walked this way, then that. I watched him through a window. He didn't see me. My heart was broken. Him an' his father was so awful, awful close. More like brothers than father an' son, they were."

"Mr. Wilson talked to him, didn't he?"

"Yes, they had a long talk. What they said, I don't know. Look out the window at the Montana House! It's jus' ablaze with lamplights. Look, you can see that filthy Johnson—an' Corcoran—through the big window. Johnson's on the left."

Corcoran and Johnson still spoke about Mel Griffin stopping to talk with Matt Wilson. "Wilson dig up his brother an' fin' two bullet holes in his head an' the jig is up," Johnson said.

"We can't allow that," Corcoran said.

"Hanford's swung over to them farmers, or I'm a hog-swazzled fool," Johnson said. "The way it 'pears to me if somebody kilt Wilson, the farmers would all cave—no leader."

Corcoran nodded.

"Why not sic Griffin against Wilson? Johnson asked.

"I doubt if Griffin could outdraw and outshoot him," Corcoran said.

Johnson grinned. "What if he plugged Griffin? What have you lost, boss?"

"Only a tin-plate gent claimin' to be a gunman," Corcoran said. "I've never seen Griffin in action."

"How come you hire him?"

"He rode in claimin' he was a fast one with a gun. Somethin' about the Tonto Basin, down in Arizona. Thought I'd give him a whirl."

"Test him against Wilson."

Corcoran said: "You're over-steppin', Rand. I'm runnin' this spread. What about you goin' against Wilson?"

"You order it and I go."

Corcoran grinned. "I'll get Griffin." he killed his drink and climbed the stairs. Griffin was in bed asleep. He stumbled in his b.v.d.s to the door. "What's up, boss?"

Corcoran went to the point. "I want you to gun down Matt Wilson, an' to kill him tonight."

"He's as good as dead," Griffin said. "Where's he now?"

"I think he's with the farmers in the hardware store."

Griffin blinked. "Hell, I can't walk in there after him. They'll cut me down like a mower cuttin' alfalfa. I'll have to wait until he gets alone, boss."

"Kill him."

Corcoran left.

Griffin slowly dressed. He put everything he owned between two blankets and rolled all into a bedroll. The time had come.

He went to the window to look down on Main Street. Farmers were dim and shadowy figures as they entered and left the hardware store. From this distance it looked as though some wobbled on underpins.

The store was bright with kerosene lamps. Harsh voices came from the open door.

Griffin went to open his window so he could hear better, but the rain had swollen the once-dry wood. He tugged and pulled. Finally he got the window half open.

Now he heard the voices of women. Despite distance, he caught a few words.

They'll kill you . . . .

You're a married man with a family . . . .

You're not a gunman. You're not going into that damned saloon . . . .

Grinning, Griffin pulled the window shut. He checked drawers and the clothes closet. He'd overlooked nothing. All his earthly possessions were in the bedroll.

Leaving the bedroll in his room, he went into the hall, carefully locking his door and checking to make sure it was locked. Were Corcoran to see that bedroll, he would instantly be suspicious.

He went down the hall toward the stairway. The girls were all in their rooms. All cribs had ribbons of lamplight under their doors. He went downstairs into the saloon.

Corcoran stood alone at the bar. Johnson shot craps with Olaf for the drinks.

"Big Dick to beat, Olaf," Johnson said.

Bar Six rode in at that moment. Slicker-clad cowpunchers suddenly appeared on rain-wet, plunging saddlestock. Hoofs slid in mud, broncs reared, cowboys went down, bootheels slamming ooze.

Five gun-hung cowpokes trooped in, gunbelts outside their slickers, their guns' butts covered with leather to keep their weapons and cartridges dry.

Corcoran said: "About time, Thaddeus."

Thaddeus was a tall, bony man of forty. "Give us the word, boss, an' we clean them out."

"They're still in the hardware store," Corcoran said, "sippin' up liquid courage. There's still time. Belly up to the bar an' name your poison, boys."

The cowboys lined up, lamplight reflecting off black and yellow oilskins. Olaf left Johnson and got to work.

One cowboy said: "My pappy got shot from behin' one dark night down in Colorady fightin' them damned nesters. I'm goin' kill me a few hoemen tonight, by hell, to make my pappy sleep better in his grave."

Griffin listened, standing alone, beyond Corcoran.

"I don't need no dead pappy to push me on, Clawson," a bony cowboy said, fondling his whiskey. "I jes' don't like sodmen. I hate them worst then I hates a cow-stealin' redskin."

Griffin had heard enough. He went out the front door and turned south to walk the length of the saloon protected by the porch roof. He came to the corner. He looked back. Nobody had followed. None in the saloon could see him.

He ducked around the corner.

He stepped from the porch's protection. Rain pelting him, hand covering his holstered weapon, he ran along the Montana House's south wall, ducked around the far corner, and came to the wooden stairway leading from the alley to the saloon's second floor.

He climbed the stairs. Soon he hurried down carrying his bedroll. Everything he owned was in that small cylinder. Of course Bart Corcoran owed him almost a month's wages, but he'd sure not stop to try to collect that. He'd get out alive.

Tank Coulee, a deep, brush-filled ravine, ran along the rimrock thirty feet west of Montana House, and he

139

followed this toward the livery stable a block north.

Buckbrush hid him. He followed a trail made by town youngsters, who had a swimming-hole deep in the coulee. Then this trail turned downward into the black depths and he hurried on, making his own trail, elation singing in him.

He was making his escape. He'd head north into Canada. He knew where Corcoran had the northern guard stationed. He'd skirt the man and, once clear of this sentinel, he'd ride hard stirrups, putting miles between him and this hell-spot.

He entered the livery barn by its rear door. He knew the hostler was in Montana House, one of Corcoran's fighters. Therefore, by all evidence, the barn should hold no humans.

A lantern, hung on a ridge beam in front, gave out a dull glow, its light protected by the roof's overhang. Dim kerosene light reflected on the glossy backs of cowponies in stalls. Horses lifted heads and looked at him, glassy eyes glistening in the yellow light.

His bronc was in the fourth stall, north end. The black gelding snorted upon seeing him. The horse hated him. He hated the horse. Most horses bucked when he crawled on them, even old, well-broken saddlers.

He worked quickly, accurately. His bridle-bit went between grass-green teeth, the headstall fitting over the ears, buckling underneath. His Navajo blanket rose to fall in place on the animal's back.

Next, his Al Furstnow kak rose, settled down and, with one motion, he caught the cinch, swinging under the bronc's belly. Rapidly, he threaded the yellow latigo strap through the cinch-ring, pulled it tight, tied it—and his mount was ready for the long trail.

Bedroll under his arm, he led the bronc out the back door, which was so low a mounted man could not ride under it. Outside, rain pelted. He'd tie his bedroll behind his cantle later.

Time was of the essence, now.

He shoved his left boot into stirrup preparatory to

lifting himself into leather and then, from behind, a harsh voice cut the rain and said: "Where you goin', Griffin?"

Mel Griffin froze, boot hanging in stirrup. Carefully, slowly, heart wild, he pulled his boot free, then turned with his hand dropping his reins and going automatically to the handle of his six-shooter, protected under his slicker.

A black, raincoat-covered figure, wide and big and tough looking, stood behind him, a rain helmet protecting its head. The front lantern cast a dim glow through the barn's back door.

The black figure stood in this yellow light. Griffin saw that the raincoat bulged in front. Evidently a .45 pointed directly toward his chest.

Griffin said: "Bart Corcoran," and his voice sounded dim and distant, even in his own ears.

"Bart Corcoran it is, Griffin. Again, where are you goin', Griffin?"

"Goin' give my cayuse a little exercise, boss."

Corcoran laughed. "In this rain? I remember you sayin' you'd kill Matt Wilson sometime tonight."

"I'll do that later."

"How much later?" Corcoran taunted.

Chapter Seventeen

Griffin's mind worked now with cold precision, the first shock gone. He'd made one big error, he realized instantly.

His gun was under his slicker. He should have belted it over the raincoat. He hadn't done this because he feared the gun's mechanism would have gotten wet.

All odds favored Corcoran. Corcoran had his pistol pointed under the black raincoat.

"You got cold boots," Corcoran said, "an' you're running out."

"No, boss, no. You read me wrong—"

Corcoran interrupted: "I'd have to kill you anyway. You saw too much out at Wilson's cabin."

"Boss, no—"

Griffin never finished his sentence. Three times the concealed .45 vomited flame and lead. The first bullet missed. By then Griffin had his hand under the slicker on his own gun's grip.

He never got to draw it.

The second lead hit him in the chest. It drove him backwards four paces. He caught his balance, aware that the shock had driven his clawing fingers from his .45's black butt.

To Mel Griffin, the tableau was a scene of unreal reality. Bart Corcoran, huge and black-robed, the flame shooting from his middle, the darkness of the Montana night, the hard sweep of driving rain—all these points added in Griffin's startled brain, but seemed to lack reality.

Corcoran's third bullet caught Griffin in the belly. It drove him back again. Griffin was aware of a thudding force, then blinding pain. He turned and ran, hunched over, for Tank Coulee.

Behind him, Corcoran's .45 belched two more times. Griffin realized the leads had missed. He knew Corcoran carried five cartridges in his .45, letting the hammer rest safely on an empty chamber.

He fell over Tank Coulee's lip. He fell straight down, then hit a talus cone, and began to roll.

He rolled over buckbrush. Wild rosebushes tore at him with long spines. He crashed over boulders. He thought he'd never stop rolling. Finally he rolled into water.

He'd reached the canyon's bottom. He was in the town swimming-hole. Hands digging mud, he crawled onto the bank. He lay there with the terror of the night slowly dying.

He was bleeding. He was dimly aware of that. His wounds, though, didn't hurt. He wondered if he were not beyond pain. He tried to sit up. He failed. He fell back again on his side.

He closed his eyes. He tried to gather his thoughts. One thought stood out: he'd have to move away from this spot. Bart Corcoran might go back to where the trail came down the cliff.

Corcoran would search for him. Yes, he had to move. Hate welled in him toward Corcoran. With hate was the desire for revenge. Somehow he'd make Corcoran pay.

But how?

He might be dying, he told himself. How could you tell whether or not you were dying? He was badly wounded. He'd already lost a lot of blood, he reasoned.

Then one name flashed into his brain: Matt Wilson.

He'd seen Bart Corcoran murder Jim Wilson. Matt Wilson said he'd kill his brother's assassin. He had to

144

get to Matt Wilson. He had to tell Matt Wilson what he knew. All of it.

Wilson would then lift his gun against Corcoran. Wilson was a heller with a cutter. Wilson would kill Corcoran.

Or would he?

Was Wilson fast enough to outdraw Corcoran? Was he the more accurate? Would he kill Corcoran before Corcoran killed him?

Griffin didn't know. Griffin could only guess. Would he be alive to see the inevitable gunfight?

Suddenly, he heard boots to the south. Corcoran had descended. Then he heard Corcoran say: "The bastard fell somewhere in this area."

"We'll find him," Rand Johnson said. "Wish we had a lantern."

"But we ain't," Corcoran said.

With difficulty, on hands and knees, Mel Griffin crawled laboriously, slowly, into the waist-high buckbrush, and within a minute or so two big black-clad figures came into view.

To Griffin's horror, they stopped on the trail no more than twenty feet to the west. Griffin stifled a groan. Pain surged through his body. He wanted to cry out. Only by sheer will-power—and a hand clenched over his open mouth—did he succeed in stifling his desire.

"He's prob'ly dead," Johnson said. "He took two of 'em, for sure. They almost knocked him down."

"My last two bullets missed, I think," Corcoran said.

Griffin suddenly decided he'd kill the two. He'd pull his gun and—for the first time, Griffin realized his holster was empty. He had lost his .45 in the canyon fall.

He wanted to sob in anger, but no sobs came. How long would these two monsters stand there and stare around looking for him, and he almost at the toes of their boots?

He was thankful for the dark night. And here in the canyon's fetid bottom the night was even darker. That much was in his favor.

Griffin heard the whirr of wings rising. Somewhere north a covey of grouse were scared from roosting-grounds.

"He's over there," Johnson said. "Them is grouse flyin'. He's scared them up."

"Come on, " Corcoran said.

The black forms disappeared. Griffin closed his eyes. He wanted to sleep despite his pain. Or was it not sleep? Was it death?

He couldn't die. He'd have to live long enough to talk to Matt Wilson. If he died before seeing Wilson, Corcoran would never pay for the bullets he'd planted in his body, Griffin realized.

Griffin got sitting up. His blood had soaked his shirt. He wondered if he'd not quit bleeding. He gathered what thoughts he could. How would he get to Wilson?

He realized that Tank Coulee now ran a small stream of rainwater. Yesterday its bottom had been tinder-dry except for the swimming-hole, which drought had been making smaller and smaller each consecutive day.

He'd wade upstream. There was another trail upward, just south of Sageville, a few rods. He'd climb it and get to the hardware store. And if Wilson were not there he'd find out where Wilson was. . .and go to him there.

The water was muddy. He slipped. He lay for a moment in the water, just his head up. Finally he had strength enough to again regain his boots. The water was cold.

Bent over, hand over the wound in his belly, he advanced, each step uncertain, wobbly. He felt nausea swarming in. He had sense enough to wade out onto the east bank into a clump of diamond willows.

Here, he fell forward. Blackness zoomed in and held him. When he opened his eyes again, dawn was streaking the rainclouds above. He had lain unconscious for some hours.

He sat up. He looked down his shirt front, for his slicker hung open. Matted blood coated his shirt. He decided to get rid of his raincoat. The slicker was just a hindrance, dragging tail against brush.

He had trouble shedding the black oilskin, but finally it lay abandoned. He had little strength. He should have been hungry, but he wasn't. He stumbled ahead, mindful of nothing but his objective—to find Matt Wilson and tell him.

After what seemed ages, he reached the upward trail. Dawn was a little brighter now, but it would have little brilliance because of the heavy skies. Rain fell in a steady, bone-chilling drizzle.

Rainwater trickled down the trail, making a long indentation. The bank was slippery. Knees wabbling, he stood trembling, studying the upward climb, doubt and fear tormenting.

Doubt claimed he'd never be able to climb to the end of that trail. Fear plagued him and screamed he'd never complete his mission.

He went to hands and knees. He'd climb like a four-legged animal, fingers clawing hand-holds, boots digging behind for purchase.

Then another fear struck him. What if Bart Corcoran—or Rand Johnson—suddenly appeared at the head of the trail, shortgun or rifle in hand? Did the pair still hunt him?

Sheer exhaustion clutched him. He fell on his face in the mud. Blackness threatened again, but finally receded. He lifted his head. He was alone in Chester's night pasture. Two ugly cows gazed at him.

"Go away," he said.

The cows lowered their horns. They returned to their cropping bunch grass. They wanted nothing to do with him.

He got to his feet. Jim Wilson's hardware store was half a block north. He started toward it. Nobody was in front of it. Had the farmers hit Montana House during the night?

No, Montana House was still there. Two figures had come out onto the porch. Despite drizzling rain Griffin recognized Rand Johnson and Bart Corcoran.

Johnson's harsh words came clearly. "Hell, Bart! That's Griffin, I tell you!"

"By damn it is! Run in for a rifle, fast."

Johnson wheeled and ran into the bar. Corcoran lifted his .45. He aimed carefully over his forearm. The gun belched flame. Mud geysered upward a hundred feet in front of Griffin, who hurried as fast as possible for the hardware store's door.

Corcoran's gun roar brought farmers from the store. They stared in amazement at Corcoran shooting at one of his gunmen. Somebody then noticed that Griffin was wounded.

"He's all bloody, men!"

Corcoran shot again. This time, he elevated his front sight. The bullet hit the plank sidewalk three feet in front of Griffin's staggering boots. Wet splinters rose.

The farmers scattered. They piled back into the store. Griffin saw Johnson break out of the Montana House, a rifle in his hands. Johnson stopped legs spread wide, on the saloon's porch.

His rifle rose, but before he could shoot, Mel Griffin had fallen into the store, out of Johnson's sight.

"Wilson? Where's Wilson?"

Doc Myers said: "He isn't here. I think he's in Jean's cafe. Who shot you, Griffin?"

"Wilson. Matt Wilson. I gotta talk to Wilson."

Young Mack Smith said: "I'll go after him," and ran out the back door. Doc Myers was on his knees beside Griffin.

"Holy Smoke," the veterinarian said.

Griffin asked: "How bad am I hurt?"

A farmer said: "Get out on the street in front, one or two of you. Corcoran shot at this man. Him an' Johnson might come an' try to kill him."

Three armed farmers went out front.

"Why'd Corcoran shoot at you?" Doc Myers asked.

Gasping, spitting blood, Mel Griffin briefly outlined what had happened, with Doc Myers cutting the man's bloody clothing from him. Finally, the two wounds lay bare.

"Will I live, Doc?"

"I don't know, Mel. Man, I'm only mortal—I'm not God. You lived this long without medical help. Maybe you'll live longer with a little scientific help."

"I gotta tell Wilson what I know."

"Tell me. Then if you die—"

"I'm not goin' to die. Not till I talk to Wilson, anyway."

"Here comes Matt now," a farmer said who stood guard at the rear door. "Jean's with him, an' so is the Widder Smith."

Matt Wilson knelt beside the wounded man. "Griffin—what is it, man?"

"Remember us talkin' out by the graveyard?"

"Yes, go on."

"You had the thing pegged right, Wilson. Even to powder burns on the window. You dig your brother up an' you'll fin' two holes in the back of his head, like you reckoned."

"Who shot him from behind?"

"Bart Corcoran. I was there. So was Rand Johnson. That's why Corcoran tried to kill me. To silence me, Wilson."

Young Mack Smith watched Matt Wilson. Not a trace of emotion touched the gambler's high-cheeked face.

Matt Wilson looked about at the stolid faces. "I want you all to bear witness as to Griffin's words."

Mel Griffin spoke to Doc Myers. "Am I goin' die, Doc?"

Doc Myers tipped his bottle. "You asked me that before. I have the same answer. I'm not God Almighty. But I got a sneakin' hunch, as tough as you are, you'll still raise a few grandkids."

Mel Griffin smiled. "I'll bet they'll be homely little tykes." He closed his eyes. "Get to work, sawbones."

Matt Wilson got slowly to his feet. He looked for a

long moment at the wounded man's bloodless face. Then he raised his head. His eyes met Jean Benson's troubled ones.

Jean asked, quietly: "What are you going to do?"

"I'm a United States citizen," Wilson said, "and any citizen can arrest another when he sees him committing a crime and there's no law officer close. I'm going to arrest Rand Johnson and Bart Corcoran."

Wilson paused.

Then he said: "and the charge will be murder."

Chapter Eighteen

Jean Benson's voice was surprisingly calm. "There are two of them, Matt. And you are only one."

"He'll not be alone," young Mack Smith said, "because I'll be with him, Miss Benson."

Wilson looked at the boy. "No," he said.

Mack Smith said: "Rand Johnson killed my father. Bart Corcoran killed your brother. You'll lift a gun against both so your brother can sleep well in his Montana grave."

Wilson listened. The farmers listened. Mrs. Smith clutched her apron, twisting the faded old cloth, Jean Benson listened.

The youth said: "I'm a man now, Matt. My father sleeps in a cold grave, too. I loved him like you loved your brother. If I don't go with you, then I go alone."

"Mack," his mother said.

Mack Smith faced his mother. "I love you, Mother. But still, I wouldn't want to live—to spend my days—under this shadow. It would be better if I were dead, too."

"I think I understand," his mother said.

Wilson saw he could do nothing. So he said: "We will both need Wilson's Man."

"He'll sit on your shoulder closest to me," young Mack Smith said.

A farmer said: "You're not doin' this alone, you two.

We're in this, too—remember?"

Wilson shook his head. "I told you once I was not a farmer, not one of you. I admire you. I sympathize with your work. At heart, I think you are foolish to even put a plow into this ground. But I'm not you and you're not me. I'll either ride out of this town or I'll stay here forever."

"I can't agree with you completely, Mr. Wilson," Russell Halversen said. "Your brother was our friend. He lent us money. He was our president. Horace Smith was our president, too. He was killed because he was that. That makes it our battle, too."

"He's right," a woman said.

Wilson said: "Listen to sense. You men have families, responsibilities. Bullets kill, bullets maim. Let's put it this way, people."

"How is that?" a man asked.

Doc Myers had Mel Griffin asleep, the sickly smell of chloroform permeating the damp air.

"This boy and I might fail. We both might get killed. If we do, and you want to, then you can move in with guns. But remember, Bar Six riders are in the saloon. They're armed and ready."

Men and women listened, yellow lamplight showing somber, wind-beaten faces. One farmer slept drunkenly in the corner. He snored loudly. The others had seemingly lost all effects of alcohol under the shock of seeing bloody and bullet torn Mel Griffin stagger in and fall.

Jean Benson turned and walked out. Mrs. Smith went with her, Matt Wilson noticed.

Wilson said: "Corcoran is the big sore, the festering sore. If we break him, kill him, they'll be without a leader, and I think they'll run— for without Corcoran, they have nothing to fight for."

"Right, right!" a woman said.

Mack Smith said: "Let's get movin', Mr. Wilson."

"Quit your old raincoat," Wilson told the youth. "Pull your pistol further ahead on your hip. That way you can reach it easier. Does your pistol lift easily?"

152

The youth went into a gunfighter's crouch, and drew. Wilson saw he was very, very slow. But which was the more necessary: speed or accuracy?

"When the trouble starts, you go down flat on your belly in the mud," Wilson told the boy, "and put your gun over your forearm. Take good aim—and then shoot."

"Johnson killed my father," the boy said.

Wilson nodded. "I take Corcoran. You take Johnson."

"Why do you want me to go into the mud, Mr. Wilson?"

Wilson was checking his gun. "Because when you're down, you make a smaller target."

"And you stand?"

"Yes."

"Then they'll direct full fire at you. I don't like that plan, sir."

Wilson tied his tie-down thongs. He looked at the boy. "You do as I say, young man, or I'll knock you flat, here and now, with my six-shooter, and you'll not be in any gunfight—you'll be in dreamland."

Wilson meant each and every word.

Young Mack Smith said: "I do as you order, sir. To the letter, Mr. Wilson."

"Better," Wilson said.

A farmer said: "I'm watchin' out the window, Mr. Wilson. Corcoran and Johnson are alone on the saloon's porch. You're takin' a wild chance-card, sir. Guns from inside might cut you down."

"If they do," Halversen said, "we start a war, Matt."

Wilson looked at Mack Smith. "Are you ready?"

"I'm ready, Mr. Wilson."

Men stepped aside. One woman crossed herself. Matt Wilson and Mack Smith moved through the group, Wilson a pace in the lead. They stepped into the gray and raw and rainy Montana dawn.

Mack Smith pulled even with Matt Wilson. "Your father was untying his team. His back was toward

Johnson. Johnson shot him from behind. I saw it, Mack."

"Why didn't you say so before?"

"Because it would have broken open pure hell. Men with wives and children would have been killed.

Mack Smith said: "I killed Walt Byron."

"I heard you'd been riding that area that day. Why did you kill him?"

Their boots sounded hollow on wet planks.

"He was in ambush waitin' to kill you, Mr. Wilson. I gave him a fair chance."

Wilson said: "Let's take to the middle of the street."

They swung out into the mud.

"I came in on him on foot, Mr. Wilson. I had him stand up. I told him to go for his gun. He did."

"Separate five feet," Wilson said.

They pulled apart.

"He had me beat, Mr. Wilson, but I took my time. He missed and I connected. I saw him die. It wasn't nice to look at."

"No death is nice," said Wilson.

Corcoran and Johnson had left the Montana House's porch. They'd moved into the middle of the mud. They had spread out. Corcoran faced Matt Wilson. Johnson faced Mack Smith.

Mack Smith asked: "Where's Wilson's Man?"

"Wilson's Man is two men now," Wilson said. "He sits on your right shoulder. And he sits on mine, too."

"Wilson's Man," the boy said.

Corcoran and Johnson were in the gunfighter's stance, hands on holstered weapons. Mack Smith and Matt Wilson also had hands on gun-grips.

Finally Wilson said: "Far enough, son. We stop now. Remember what I told you, please."

"I remember, Mr. Wilson."

"Good boy, Mack."

Wilson's voice was tight. He thought of Jean Benson. He thought of Copacabana's white beach, Sugarloaf towering behind. Four gunhung men faced each other.

Wilson spoke to Corcoran. "You ambushed my brother. You shot him through the back of the head through that window. Johnson was with you. So was Griffin. Griffin told me."

Corcoran said: "Griffin is a bum, nothin' more. His word doesn't count in a court of law."

Wilson spoke to Rand Johnson without looking at the man. "You murdered Horace Smith. I saw you shoot him in the back."

"Only the word of a drifter against mine," Johnson said.

Corcoran asked: "What's your play, tinhorn?"

"As citizens, Mack Smith and I are arresting you two —and the charge is murder."

Corcoran laughed harshly. "Do you think we'll go with you?"

"You go peacefully, or we take you," Matt Wilson said.

Nobody spoke again. All had been said. The time had arrived. The rain fell. Matt Wilson saw Bart Corcoran move his left hand slightly. Corcoran had given the signal.

Then the guns left leather.

Then the guns roared.

Now an invisible rider rode in between the four snarling guns. He was dressed from head to toe in funeral black. He rode a black horse.

Bullets went through him. Bullets went through his horse.

Neither felt them.

The rider's name was Death.

Death looked at Bart Corcoran who had fallen forward on his side, smoking gun lying in a water puddle. Wilson's bullets had broken the gold watch-chain, driving heavy links back into Corcoran's heart.

Death said: "Corcoran, you come with me."

Death then looked at Randolf Johnson, who lay face down in the mud, and Death said: "Johnson, you come with me."

Death then looked at young Mack Smith.

Mack Smith knelt on one knee, gun lying in a puddle, his right hand clutching his bloody left shoulder, pain etched deeply on his boyish face, and Death said: "Wilson taught you well. Time passes on swift eagle wings. Before you know it you will be old. Then I will come for you, Mack Smith."

Death looked at Matt Wilson.

Matt Wilson had holstered his hot gun home against his thigh. He was walking toward the woman he loved. And Jean Benson had dropped her Winchester .30-30.

She came running toward him and the glory of her was in her tear-filled eyes, the sunshine of her in her glorious body.

Death said: "Wilson, you stay here."

Then Death rode away and Corcoran and Johnson followed into eternity. Death glanced upward.

Above, Death saw the high-cheekboned face of a dark-eyed, dark-haired woman.

Death watched her.

SUNDANCE #38: DRUMFIRE
By Peter McCurtin

PRICE: $1.95 LB976
CATEGORY: Western

SUNDANCE AND GERONIMO!

Apache chief Geronimo was released from a Florida prison camp on the condition that he must become a farmer in Oklahoma. It was up to Sundance to get the hated chief there alive. Their journey was destined for blood.

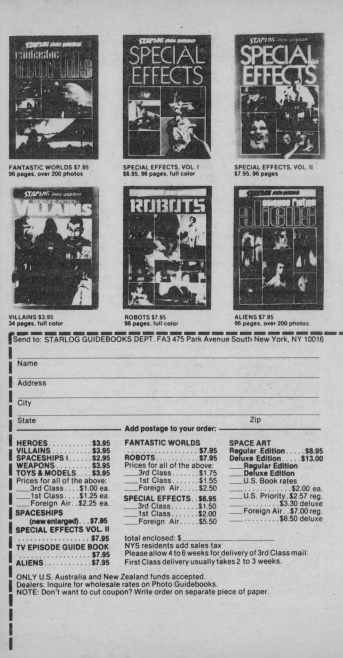